"That's silly," Aran broke in. "What good is a glass dagger?"

The Warlock raised the knife high, and brought it down hard on Aran's chest.

Aran screamed. He *had* felt it! A whisper of sensation, a slight ghostly tug—the knife was an insubstantial shadow. But there *was* a knife in Aran the Peacemonger's heart! The hilt stood up out of his chest!

The Warlock muttered low and fast. The glass hilt faded and was gone.

"It's easy to make glass invisible. It's still in your heart," said the Warlock. "But don't worry about it. Don't give it a thought. Nobody will notice. Only be sure to spend the rest of your life in *mana*-rich territory. Because if you ever walk into a place where magic doesn't work—well, it'll reappear, that's all . . ."

THE FLIGHT
OF THE HORSE

Larry Niven

A Del Rey Book

BALLANTINE BOOKS • NEW YORK

DEDICATION

There was a time when I had to tell a story to someone, verbally, to know if it was worth writing. I had to know where the story was confused, or what points to explain fully, or whether I had made my point, or even whether I had a point to make. I bent a lot of ears in those days.

This book is dedicated to those who were willing to listen. Starting with my brother Mike.

Contents

Contents

The Flight
of the Horse

THE FLIGHT OF THE HORSE

The year was 750AA (AnteAtomic) or 1200 AD (Anno Domini), approximately. Hanville Svetz stepped out of the extension cage and looked about him.

To Svetz the atomic bomb was eleven hundred years old and the horse was a thousand years dead. It was his first trip into the past. His training didn't count; it had not included actual time travel, which cost several million commercials a shot. Svetz was groggy from the peculiar gravitational side effects of time travel. He was high on pre-industrial-age air, and drunk on his own sense of destiny; while at the same time he was not really convinced that he had *gone* anywhere. Or anywhen. Trade joke.

He was not carrying the anaesthetic rifle. He had come to get a horse; he had not expected to meet one at the door. How big was a horse? Where were horses found? Consider what the Institute had had to go on: a few pictures in a salvaged children's book, and an old legend, not to be trusted, that the horse had once been used as a kind of animated vehicle!

In an empty land beneath an overcast sky, Svetz braced himself with one hand on the curved flank of the extension cage. His head was spinning. It took him several seconds to realize that he was looking at a horse.

It stood fifteen yards away, regarding Svetz with large intelligent brown eyes. It was much larger than he had expected. Further, the horse in the picture book had had a

1

glossy brown pelt with a short mane, while the beast now facing Svetz was pure white, with a mane that flowed like a woman's long hair. There were other differences . . . but no matter, the beast matched the book too well to be anything but a horse.

To Svetz it seemed that the horse watched him, waited for him to realize what was happening. Then, while Svetz wasted more time wondering why he wasn't holding a rifle, the horse laughed, turned, and departed. It disappeared with astonishing speed.

Svetz began to shiver. Nobody had warned him that the horse might have been sentient! Yet the beast's mocking laugh had sounded far too human.

Now he knew. He was deep, deep in the past.

Not even the horse was as convincing as the emptiness the horse had left behind. No reaching apartment towers clawed the horizon. No contrails scratched the sky. The world was trees and flowers and rolling grassland, innocent of men.

The silence— It was as if Svetz had gone deaf. He had heard no sound since the laughter of the horse. In the year 1100 PostAtomic, such silence could have been found nowhere on Earth. Listening, Svetz knew at last that he had reached the British Isles before the coming of civilization. He had traveled in time.

The extension cage was the part of the time machine that did the traveling. It had its own air supply, and needed it while being pushed through time. But not here. Not before civilization's dawn; not when the air had never been polluted by fission wastes and the combustion of coal, hydrocarbons, tobaccos, wood, et al.

Now, retreating in panic from that world of the past to the world of the extension cage, Svetz nonetheless left the door open behind him.

2

He felt better inside the cage. Outside was an unexplored planet, made dangerous by ignorance. Inside the cage it was no different from a training mission. Svetz had spent hundreds of hours in a detailed mockup of this cage, with a computer running the dials. There had even been artificial gravity to simulate the peculiar side effects of motion in time.

By now the horse would have escaped. But he now knew its size, and he knew there were horses in the area. To business, then . . .

Svetz took the anaesthetic rifle from where it was clamped to the wall. He loaded it with what he guessed was the right size of soluble crystalline anaesthetic needle. The box held several different sizes, the smallest of which would knock a shrew harmlessly unconscious, the largest of which would do the same for an elephant. He slung the rifle and stood up.

The world turned grey. Svetz caught a wall clamp to stop himself from falling.

The cage had stopped moving twenty minutes ago. He shouldn't still be dizzy! —But it had been a long trip. Never before had the Institute for Temporal Research pushed a cage beyond zero PA. A long trip and a strange one, with gravity pulling Svetz's mass uniformly toward Svetz's navel . . .

When his head cleared, he turned to where other equipment was clamped to a wall.

The flight stick was a lift field generator and power source built into five feet of pole, with a control ring at one end, a brush discharge at the other, and a bucket seat and seat belt in the middle. Compact even for Svetz's age, the flight stick was a spinoff from the spaceflight industries.

But it still weighed thirty pounds with the motor off. Getting it out of the clamps took all his strength. Svetz felt queasy, very queasy.

3

He bent to pick up the flight stick, and abruptly realized that he was about to faint.

He hit the door button and fainted.

"We don't know where on Earth you'll wind up," Ra Chen had told him. Ra Chen was the Director of the Institute for Temporal Research, a large round man with gross, exaggerated features and a permanent air of disapproval. "That's because we can't focus on a particular time of day—or on a particular year, for that matter. You won't appear underground or inside anything because of energy considerations. If you come out a thousand feet in the air, the cage won't fall; it'll settle slowly, using up energy with a profligate disregard for our budget . . ."

And Svetz had dreamed that night, vividly. Over and over his extension cage appeared inside solid rock, exploded with a roar and a blinding flash.

"Officially the horse is for the Bureau of History," Ra Chen had said. "In practice it's for the Secretary-General, for his twenty-eighth birthday. Mentally he's about six years old, you know. The royal family's getting a bit inbred these days. We managed to send him a picture book we picked up in 130 PA, and now the lad wants a horse . . ."

Svetz had seen himself being shot for treason, for the crime of listening to such talk.

". . . Otherwise we'd never have gotten the appropriation for this trip. It's in a good cause. We'll do some cloning from the horse before we send the original to the UN. Then—well, genes are a code, and codes can be broken. Get us a male, and we'll make all the horses anyone could want."

But why would anyone want even one horse? Svetz had studied a computer duplicate of the child's picture book that an agent had pulled from a ruined house a thousand years ago. The horse did not impress him.

Ra Chen, however, terrified him.

"We've never sent anyone this far back," Ra Chen had told him the night before the mission, when it was too late to back out with honor. "Keep that in mind. If something goes wrong, don't count on the rule book. Don't count on your instruments. Use your head. Your head, Svetz. Gods know it's little enough to depend on . . ."

Svetz had not slept in the hours before departure.

"You're scared stiff," Ra Chen had commented just before Svetz entered the extension cage. "And you can hide it, Svetz. I think I'm the only one who's noticed. That's why I picked you, because you can be terrified and go ahead anyway. Don't come back without a horse . . ."

The Director's voice grew louder. "Not without a horse, Svetz. Your *head,* Svetz, your HEAD . . ."

Svetz sat up convulsively. The air! Slow death if he didn't close the door! But the door was closed, and Svetz was sitting on the floor holding his head, which hurt.

The air system had been transplanted intact, complete with dials, from a martian sandboat. The dials read normally, of course, since the cage was sealed.

Svetz nerved himself to open the door. As the sweet, rich air of twelfth-century britain rushed in, Svetz held his breath and watched the dials change. Presently he closed the door and waited, sweating, while the air system replaced the heady poison with its own safe, breathable mixture.

When next he left the extension cage, carrying the flight stick, Svetz was wearing another spinoff from the interstellar exploration industries. It was a balloon, and he wore it over his head. It was also a selectively permeable membrane, intended to pass certain gasses in and others out, to make a breathing-air mixture inside.

It was nearly invisible except at the rim. There, where light was refracted most severely, the balloon showed as a narrow golden circle enclosing Svetz's head. The effect was not unlike a halo as shown in medieval paintings. But Svetz didn't know about medieval paintings.

He wore also a simple white robe, undecorated, constricted at the waist, otherwise falling in loose folds. The Institute thought that such a garment was least likely to violate taboos of sex or custom. The trade kit dangled loose from his sash: a heat-and-pressure gadget, a pouch of corundum, small phials of additives for color.

Lastly he wore a hurt and baffled look. How was it that he could not breathe the clean air of his own past?

The air of the cage was the air of Svetz's time, and was nearly four percent carbon dioxide. The air of 750 Ante-Atomic held barely a tenth of that. Man was a rare animal here and now. He had breathed little air, he had destroyed few green forests, he had burnt scant fuel since the dawn of time.

But industrial civilization meant combustion. Combustion meant carbon dioxide thickening in the atmosphere many times faster than the green plants could turn it back to oxygen. Svetz was at the far end of two thousand years of adaptation to air rich in CO_2.

It takes a concentration of carbon dioxide to trigger the autonomic nerves in the lymph glands in a man's left armpit. Svetz had fainted because he wasn't breathing.

So now he wore a balloon, and felt rejected.

He straddled the flight stick and twisted the control knob on the fore end. The stick lifted under him, and he wriggled into place on the bucket seat. He twisted the knob further.

He drifted upward like a toy balloon.

He floated over a lovely land, green and untenanted, beneath a pearl-grey sky empty of contrails. Presently he found a crumbling wall. He turned to follow it.

He would follow the wall until he found a settlement. If the old legend was true—and, Svetz reflected, the horse had certainly been *big* enough to drag a vehicle—then he would find horses wherever he found men.

6

Presently it became obvious that a road ran along the wall. There the dirt was flat and bare and consistently wide enough for a walking man, whereas elsewhere the land rose and dipped and tilted. Hard dirt did not a freeway make; but Svetz got the point.

He followed the road, floating at a height of ten meters. There was a man in worn brown garments. Hooded and barefoot, he walked the road with patient exhaustion, propping himself with a staff. His back was to Svetz.

Svetz thought to dip toward him to ask concerning horses. He refrained. With no way to know where the cage would alight, he had learned no ancient languages at all.

He thought of the trade kit he carried, intended not for communication, but instead of communication. It had never been field-tested. In any case it was not for casual encounters. The pouch of corundum was too small.

Svetz heard a yell from below. He looked down in time to see the man in brown running like the wind, his staff forgotten, his fatigue likewise.

"Something scared him," Svetz decided. But he could see nothing fearful. Something small but deadly, then.

The Institute estimated that man had exterminated more than a thousand species of mammal and bird and insect—some casually, some with malice—between now and the distant present. In this time and place there was no telling what might be a threat. Svetz shuddered. The brown man with the hairy face might well have run from a stinging thing destined to kill Hanville Svetz.

Impatiently Svetz upped the speed of his flight stick. The mission was taking far too long. Who would have guessed that centers of population would have been so far apart?

Half an hour later, shielded from the wind by a paraboloid force field, Svetz was streaking down the road at sixty miles per hour.

His luck had been incredibly bad. Wherever he had chanced across a human being, that person had been just leaving the vicinity. And he had found no centers of population.

Once he had noticed an unnatural stone outcropping high on a hill. No law of geology known to Svetz could have produced such an angular, flat-sided monstrosity. Curious, he had circled above it—and had abruptly realized that the thing was hollow, riddled with rectangular holes.

A dwelling for men? He didn't want to believe it. Living within the hollows of such a thing would be like living underground. But men tend to build at right angles, and this thing was *all* right angles.

Below the hollowed stone structure were rounded, hairy-looking hummocks of dried grass, each with a man-sized door. Obviously they must be nests for very large insects. Svetz had left that place quickly.

The road rounded a swelling green hill ahead of him. Svetz followed, slowing.

A hilltop spring sent a stream bubbling downhill to break the road. Something large was drinking at the stream.

Svetz jerked to a stop in midair. *Open water: deadly poison.* He would have been hard put to say which had startled him more: the horse, or the fact that it had just committed suicide.

The horse looked up and saw him.

It was the same horse. White as milk, with a flowing abundance of snowy mane and tail, it almost had to be the horse that had laughed at Svetz and run. Svetz recognized the malignance in its eyes, in the moment before it turned its back.

But how could it have arrived so fast?

Svetz was reaching for the gun when the situation turned upside down.

The girl was young, surely no more than sixteen. Her

8

hair was long and dark and plaited in complex fashion. Her dress, of strangely stiff blue fabric, reached from her neck to her ankles. She was seated in the shadow of a tree, on dark cloth spread over the dark earth. Svetz had not noticed her, might never have noticed her . . .

But the horse walked up to her, folded its legs in alternate pairs, and laid its ferocious head in her lap.

The girl had not yet seen Svetz.

"Xenophilia!" Svetz snarled the worst word he could think of. Svetz hated aliens.

The horse obviously belonged to the girl. He could not simply shoot it and take it. It would have to be purchased . . . somehow.

He needed time to think! And there was no time, for the girl might look up at any moment. Baleful brown eyes watched him as he dithered . . .

He dared waste no more time searching the countryside for a wild horse. There was an uncertainty, a Finagle factor in the math of time travel. It manifested itself as an uncertainty in the energy of a returning extension cage, and it increased with time. Let Svetz linger too long, and he could be roasted alive in the returning cage.

Moreover, the horse had drunk open water. It would die, and soon, unless Svetz could return it to 1100 PostAtomic. Thus the beast's removal from this time could not change the history of Svetz's own world. It was a good choice . . . if he could conquer his fear of the beast.

The horse was tame. Young and slight as she was, the girl had no trouble controlling it. What was there to fear?

But there was its natural weaponry . . . of which Ra Chen's treacherous picture book had shown no sign. Svetz surmised that later generations routinely removed it before the animals were old enough to be dangerous. He should have come a few centuries later . . .

And there was the look in its eye. The horse hated Svetz, and it knew Svetz was afraid.

Could he shoot it from ambush?

No. The girl would worry if her pet collapsed without reason. She would be unable to concentrate on what Svetz was trying to tell her.

He would have to work with the animal watching him. If the girl couldn't control it—or if he lost her trust—Svetz had little doubt that the horse would kill him.

The horse looked up as Svetz approached, but made no other move. The girl watched too, her eyes round with wonder. She called something that must have been a question.

Svetz smiled back and continued his approach. He was a foot above the ground, and gliding at dead slow. Riding the world's only flying machine, he looked impressive as all hell, and knew it.

The girl did not smile back. She watched warily. Svetz was within yards of her when she scrambled to her feet.

He stopped the flight stick at once and let it settle. Smiling placatorily, he removed the heat-and-pressure device from his sash. He moved with care. The girl was on the verge of running.

The trade kit was a pouch of corundum, Al_2O_3, several phials of additives, and the heat-and-pressure gadget. Svetz poured corundum into the chamber, added a dash of chromic oxide, and used the plunger. The cylinder grew warm. Presently Svetz dropped a pigeon's-blood star ruby into his hand, rolled it in his fingers, held it to the sun. It was red as dark blood, with a blazing white six-pointed star.

It was almost too hot to hold.

Stupid! Svetz held his smile rigid. Ra Chen should have warned him! What would she think when she felt the gem's unnatural heat? What trickery would she suspect?

But he had to chance it. The trade kit was all he had.

He bent and rolled the gem to her across the damp ground.

She stooped to pick it up. One hand remained on the horse's neck, calming it. Svetz noticed the rings of yellow metal around her wrist; and he also noticed the dirt.

She held the gem high, looked into its deep red fire.

"Ooooh," she breathed. She smiled at Svetz in wonder and delight. Svetz smiled back, moved two steps nearer, and rolled her a yellow sapphire.

How had he twice chanced on the same horse? Svetz never knew. But he soon knew how it had arrived before him . . .

He had given the girl three gems. He held three more in his hand while he beckoned her onto the flight stick. She shook her head; she would not go. Instead she mounted the animal.

She and the horse, they watched Svetz for his next move.

Svetz capitulated. He had expected the horse to follow the girl while the girl rode behind him on the flight stick. But if they both followed Svetz it would be the same.

The horse stayed to one side and a little behind Svetz's flight stick. It did not seem inconvenienced by the girl's weight. Why should it be? It must have been bred for the task. Svetz notched his speed higher, to find how fast he could conveniently move.

Faster he flew, and faster. The horse must have a limit . . .

He was up to eighty before he quit. The girl lay flat along the animal's back, hugging its neck to protect her face from the wind. But the horse ran on, daring Svetz with its eyes.

How to describe such motion? Svetz had never seen ballet. He knew how machinery moved, and this wasn't it. All he could think of was a man and a woman making love. Slippery-smooth rhythmic motion, absolute single-minded purpose, motion for the pleasure of motion. It was terrible in its beauty, the flight of the horse.

The word for such running must have died with the horse itself.

The horse would never have tired, but the girl did. She tugged on the animal's mane, and it stopped. Svetz gave her the jewels he held, made four more and gave her one.

She was crying from the wind, crying and smiling as she took the jewels. Was she smiling for the jewels, or for the joy of the ride? Exhausted, panting, she lay with her back against the warm, pulsing flank of the resting animal. Only her hand moved, as she ran her fingers repeatedly through its silver mane. The horse watched Svetz with malevolent brown eyes.

The girl was homely. It wasn't just the jarring lack of makeup. There was evidence of vitamin starvation. She was short, less than five feet in height, and thin. There were marks of childhood disease. But happiness glowed behind her homely face, and it made her almost passable, as she clutched the corundum stones.

When she seemed rested, Svetz remounted. They went on.

He was almost out of corundum when they reached the extension cage. There it was that he ran into trouble.

The girl had been awed by Svetz's jewels, and by Svetz himself, possibly because of his height or his ability to fly. But the extension cage scared her. Svetz couldn't blame her. The side with the door in it was no trouble: just a seamless spherical mirror. But the other side blurred away in a direction men could not visualize. It had scared Svetz spitless the first time he saw the time machine in action.

He could buy the horse from her, shoot it here and pull it inside, using the flight stick to float it. But it would be so much easier if . . .

It was worth a try. Svetz used the rest of his corundum.

Then he walked into the extension cage, leaving a trail of colored corundum beads behind him.

He had worried because the heat-and-pressure device would not produce facets. The stones all came out shaped like miniature hen's-eggs. But he was able to vary the color, using chromic oxide for red and ferric oxide for yellow and titanium for blue; and he could vary the pressure planes, to produce cat's-eyes or star gems at will. He left a trail of small stones, red and yellow and blue . . .

And the girl followed, frightened, but unable to resist the bait. By now she had nearly filled a handkerchief with the stones. The horse followed her into the extension cage.

Inside, she looked at the four stones in Svetz's hand: one of each color, red and yellow and light blue and black, the largest he could make. He pointed to the horse, then to the stones.

The girl agonized. Svetz perspired. She didn't want to give up the horse . . . and Svetz was out of corundum . . .

She nodded, one swift jerk of her chin. Quickly, before she could change her mind, Svetz poured the stones into her hand. She clutched the hoard to her bosom and ran out of the cage, sobbing.

The horse stood up to follow.

Svetz swung the rifle and shot it. A bead of blood appeared on the animal's neck. It shied back, then sighted on Svetz along its natural bayonet.

Poor kid, Svetz thought as he turned to the door. But she'd have lost the horse anyway. It had sucked polluted water from an open stream. Now he need only load the flight stick aboard . . .

Motion caught the corner of his eye.

A false assumption can be deadly. Svetz had not waited for the horse to fall. It was with something of a shock that he realized the truth. The beast wasn't about to fall. It was about to spear him like a cocktail shrimp.

He hit the door button and dodged.

Exquisitely graceful, exquisitely sharp, the spiral horn

13

slammed into the closing door. The animal turned like white lightning in the confines of the cage, and again Svetz leapt for his life.

The point missed him by half an inch. It plunged past him and into the control board, through the plastic panel and into the wiring beneath.

Something sparkled and something sputtered.

The horse was taking careful aim, sighting along the spear in its forehead. Svetz did the only thing he could think of. He pulled the home-again lever.

The horse screamed as it went into free fall. The horn, intended for Svetz's navel, ripped past his ear and tore his breathing-balloon wide open.

Then gravity returned; but it was the peculiar gravity of an extension cage moving forward through time. Svetz and the horse were pulled against the padded walls. Svetz sighed in relief.

He sniffed again in disbelief. The smell was strong and strange, like nothing Svetz had ever smelled before. The animal's terrible horn must have damaged the air plant. Very likely he was breathing poison. If the cage didn't return in time . . .

But would it return at all? It might be going anywhere, anywhen, the way that ivory horn had smashed through anonymous wiring. They might come out at the end of time, when even the black infrasuns gave not enough heat to sustain life.

There might not even be a future to return to. He had left the flight stick. How would it be used? What would they make of it, with its control handle at one end and the brush-style static discharge at the other and the saddle in the middle? Perhaps the girl would try to use it. He could visualize her against the night sky, in the light of a full moon . . . and how would that change history?

The horse seemed on the verge of apoplexy. Its sides heaved, its eyes rolled wildly. Probably it was the cabin air, thick with carbon dioxide. Again, it might be the poison the horse had sucked from an open stream.

Gravity died. Svetz and the horse tumbled in free fall, and the horse queasily tried to gore him.

Gravity returned, and Svetz, who was ready for it, landed on top. Someone was already opening the door.

Svetz took the distance in one bound. The horse followed, screaming with rage, intent on murder. Two men went flying as it charged out into the Institute control center.

"It doesn't take anaesthetics!" Svetz shouted over his shoulder. The animal's agility was hampered here among the desks and lighted screens, and it was probably drunk on hyperventilation. It kept stumbling into desks and men. Svetz easily stayed ahead of the slashing horn.

A full panic was developing . . .

"We couldn't have done it without Zeera," Ra Chen told him much later. "Your idiot tanj horse had the whole Center terrorized. All of a sudden it went completely tame, walked up to that frigid bitch Zeera and let her lead it away."

"Did you get it to the hospital in time?"

Ra Chen nodded gloomily. Gloom was his favorite expression and was no indication of his true feelings. "We found over fifty unknown varieties of bacteria in the beast's bloodstream. Yet it hardly looked sick! It looked healthy as a . . . healthy as a . . . it must have tremendous stamina. We managed to save not only the horse, but most of the bacteria too, for the Zoo."

Svetz was sitting up in a hospital bed, with his arm up to the elbow in a diagnostician. There was always the chance that he too had located some long-extinct bacterium. He shifted uncomfortably, being careful not to move the wrong arm and asked, "Did you ever find an anaesthetic that worked?"

"Nope. Sorry about that, Svetz. We still don't know why your needles didn't work. The tanj horse is simply immune to tranks of any kind.

"Incidentally, there was nothing wrong with your air plant. You were smelling the horse."

"I wish I'd known that. I thought I was dying."

"It's driving the interns crazy, that smell. And we can't seem to get it out of the Center." Ra Chen sat down on the edge of the bed. "What bothers me is the horn on its forehead. The horse in the picture book had no horns."

"No, sir."

"Then it must be a different species. It's not really a horse, Svetz. We'll have to send you back. It'll break our budget, Svetz."

"I disagree, sir—"

"Don't be so tanj polite."

"Then don't be so tanj stupid, sir." Svetz was *not* going back for another horse. "People who kept tame horses must have developed the habit of cutting off the horn when the animal was a pup. Why not? We all saw how dangerous that horn is. Much too dangerous for a domestic animal."

"Then why does our horse have a horn?"

"That's why I thought it was wild, the first time I saw it. I suppose they didn't start cutting off horns until later in history."

Ra Chen nodded in gloomy satisfaction. "I thought so too. Our problem is that the Secretary-General is barely bright enough to notice that his horse has a horn, and the picture-book horse doesn't. He's bound to blame me."

"Mmm." Svetz wasn't sure what was expected of him.

"I'll have to have the horn amputated."

"Somebody's bound to notice the scar," said Svetz.

"Tanj it, you're right. I've got enemies at court. They'd

be only too happy to claim I'd mutilated the Secretary-General's pet." Ra Chen glared at Svetz. "All right, let's hear *your* idea."

Svetz was busy regretting. Why had he spoken? His vicious, beautiful horse, tamely docked of its killer horn . . . He had found the thought repulsive. His impulse had betrayed him. What could they do but remove the horn?

He had it. "Change the picture book, not the horse. A computer could duplicate the book in detail, but with a horn on every horse. Use the Institute computer, then wipe the tape afterward."

Morosely thoughtful, Ra Chen said, "That might work. I know someone who could switch the books." He looked up from under bushy black brows. "Of course, you'd have to keep your mouth shut."

"Yes, sir."

"Don't forget." Ra Chen got up. "When you get out of the diagnostician, you start a four-week vacation."

"I'm sending you back for one of these," Ra Chen told him four weeks later. He opened the bestiary. "We picked up the book in a public park around ten PostAtomic; left the kid who was holding it playing with a corundum egg."

Svetz examined the picture. "That's *ugly*. That's really ugly. You're trying to balance the horse, right? The horse was so beautiful, you've got to have one of these or the universe goes off balance."

Ra Chen closed his eyes in pain. "Just go get us the Gila monster, Svetz. The Secretary-General wants a Gila monster."

"How big is it?"

They both looked at the illustration. There was no way to tell.

"From the looks of it, we'd better use the *big* extension cage."

Svetz barely made it back that time. He was suffering from total exhaustion and extensive second-degree burns. The thing he brought back was thirty feet long, had vestigial batlike wings, breathed fire, and didn't look very much like the illustration; but it was as close as anything he'd found.

The Secretary-General loved it.

LEVIATHAN!

Two men stood on one side of a thick glass wall.

"You'll be airborne," Svetz's beefy red-faced boss was saying. "We made some improvements in the small extension cage while you were in the hospital. You can hover it, or fly it at up to fifty miles per hour, or let it fly itself; there's a constant-altitude setting. Your field of vision is total. We've made the shell of the extension cage completely transparent."

On the other side of the thick glass, something was trying to kill them. It was forty feet long from nose to tail and was equipped with vestigial batlike wings. Otherwise it was built something like a slender lizard. It screamed and scratched at the glass with murderous claws.

The sign on the glass read:

GILA MONSTER
Retrieved from the year 1230 AnteAtomic, approximately, from the region of China, Earth. EXTINCT.

"You'll be well out of his reach," said Ra Chen.

"Yes, sir." Svetz stood with his arms folded about him, as if he had a chill. He was being sent after the biggest animal that had ever lived; and Svetz was afraid of animals.

"For Science's sake! What are you worried about, Svetz? It's only a big fish!"

"Yes, sir. You said that about the Gila monster. It's just an extinct lizard, you said."

"We only had a drawing in a children's book to go by. How could we know it would be so big?"

The Gila monster drew back from the glass. It inhaled hugely, took aim—yellow and orange flame spewed from its nostrils and played across the glass. Svetz squeaked and jumped for cover.

"He can't get through," said Ra Chen.

Svetz picked himself up. He was a slender, small-boned man with pale skin, light blue eyes, and very fine ash-blond hair. "How could we know it would breathe fire?" he mimicked. "That lizard almost *cremated* me. I spent four months in the hospital as it was. And what really burns me is, he looks less like the drawing every time I see him. Sometimes I wonder if I didn't get the wrong animal."

"What's the difference, Svetz? The Secretary-General loved him. That's what counts."

"Yes, sir. Speaking of the Secretary-General, what does he want with a sperm whale? He's got a horse, he's got a Gila monster—"

"That's a little complicated." Ra Chen grimaced. "Palace politics! It's *always* complicated. Right now, Svetz, somewhere in the United Nations Palace, a hundred plots are in various stages of development. And every last one of them involves getting the attention of the Secretary-General, and *holding* it. Keeping his attention isn't easy."

Svetz nodded. Everybody knew about the Secretary-General.

The family that had ruled the United Nations for seven hundred years was somewhat inbred.

The Secretary-General was twenty-eight years old. He was a happy person; he loved animals and flowers and pictures and people. Pictures of planets and multiple star systems made him clap his hands and coo with delight; and so the Institute for Space Research was mighty in the

United Nations government. But he liked extinct animals too.

"Someone managed to convince the Secretary-General that he wants the largest animal on Earth. The idea may have been to take us down a peg or two," said Ra Chen. "Someone may think we're getting too big a share of the budget.

"By the time I got onto it, the Secretary-General wanted a brontosaur. We'd never have gotten him that. No extension cage will reach that far."

"Was it your idea to get him a sperm whale, sir?"

"Yah. It wasn't easy to persuade him. Sperm whales have been extinct for so long that we don't even have pictures. All I had to show him was a crystal sculpture from Archeology—dug out of the Steuben Glass Building —and a Bible and a dictionary. I managed to convince him that Leviathan and the sperm whale were one and the same."

"That's not strictly true." Svetz had read a computer-produced condensation of the Bible. The condensation had ruined the plot, in Svetz's opinion. "Leviathan could be anything big and destructive, even a horde of locusts."

"Thank Science you weren't there to help, Svetz! The issue was confused enough. Anyway, I promised the Secretary-General the largest animal that ever lived on Earth. All the literature says that that animal was a sperm whale. There were sperm whale herds all over the oceans as recently as the first century Ante Atomic. You shouldn't have any trouble finding one."

"In twenty minutes?"

Ra Chen looked startled. "What?"

"If I try to keep the big extension cage in the past for more than twenty minutes, I'll never be able to bring it home. The—"

"I know that."

"—uncertainty factor in the energy constants—"

"Svetz—"

"—blow the Institute right off the map."

"We thought of that, Svetz. You'll go back in the small extension cage. When you find a whale, you'll signal the big extension cage."

"Signal it how?"

"We've found a way to send a simple on-off pulse through time. Let's go back to the Institute and I'll show you."

Malevolent golden eyes watched them through the glass as they walked away.

The extension cage was the part of the time machine that did the moving. Within its transparent shell, Svetz seemed to ride a flying armchair equipped with an airplane passenger's lunch tray; except that the lunch tray was covered with lights and buttons and knobs and crawling green lines. He was somewhere off the east coast of North America, in or around the year 100 Ante Atomic or 1845 Anno Domini. The inertial calendar was not particularly accurate.

Svetz skimmed low over water the color of lead, beneath a sky the color of slate. But for the rise and fall of the sea, he might almost have been suspended in an enormous sphere painted half light, half dark. He let the extension cage fly itself, twenty meters above the water, while he watched the needle on the NAI, the Nervous Activities Indicator.

Hunting Leviathan.

His stomach was uneasy. Svetz had thought he was adjusting to the peculiar gravitational side effects of time travel. But apparently not.

At least he would not be here long.

On this trip he was not looking for a mere forty-foot Gila monster. Now he hunted the largest animal that had ever lived. A most conspicuous beast. And now he had a life-seeking instrument, the NAI . . .

The needle jerked hard over, and trembled.

Was it a whale? But the needle was trembling in apparent indecision. A cluster of sources, then. Svetz looked in the direction indicated.

A clipper ship, winged with white sail, long and slender and graceful as hell. Crowded, too, Svetz guessed. Many humans, closely packed, would affect the NAI in just that manner. A sperm whale—a single center of complex nervous activity—would attract the needle as violently, without making it jerk about like that.

The ship would interfere with reception. Svetz turned east and away; but not without regret. The ship was beautiful.

The uneasiness in Svetz's belly was getting worse, not better.

Endless grey-green water, rising and falling beneath Svetz's flying armchair.

Enlightenment came like something clicking in his head. *Seasick.* On automatic, the extension cage matched its motion to the surface over which it flew; and that surface was heaving in great dark swells.

No wonder his stomach was uneasy! Svetz grinned and reached for the manual controls.

The NAI needle suddenly jerked hard over. A bite! thought Svetz, and he looked off to the right. No sign of a ship. And submarines hadn't been invented yet. Had they? No, of course they hadn't.

The needle was rock-steady.

Svetz flipped the call button.

The source of the tremendous NAI signal was off to his right, and moving. Svetz turned to follow it. It would be minutes before the call signal reached the Institute for Temporal Research and brought the big extension cage with its weaponry for hooking Leviathan.

Many years ago, Ra Chen had dreamed of rescuing the Library at Alexandria from Caesar's fire. For this purpose he had built the big extension cage. Its door was a gaping iris, big enough to be loaded while the Library was actually burning. Its hold, at a guess, was at least twice large enough to hold all the scrolls in that ancient Library.

The big cage had cost a fortune in government money. It had failed to go back beyond 400 AA, or 1550 AD. The books burned at Alexandria were still lost to history, or at least to historians.

Such a boondoggle would have broken other men. Somehow Ra Chen had survived the blow to his reputation.

He had pointed out the changes to Svetz after they returned from the Zoo. "We've fitted the cage out with heavy duty stunners and antigravity beams. You'll operate them by remote control. Be careful not to let the stun beam touch you. It would kill even a sperm whale if you held it on him for more than a few seconds, and it'd kill a man instantly. Other than that you should have no problems."

It was at that moment that Svetz's stomach began to hurt.

"Our major change is the call button. It will actually send us a signal through time, so that we can send the big extension cage back to you. We can land it right beside you, no more than a few minutes off. That took considerable research, Svetz. The Treasury raised our budget for this year so that we could get that whale."

Svetz nodded.

"Just be sure you've got a whale before you call for the big extension cage."

Now, twelve hundred years earlier, Svetz followed an underwater source of nervous impulse. The signal was intensely powerful. It could not be anything smaller than an adult bull sperm whale.

A shadow formed in the air to his right. Svetz watched it take shape: a great grey-blue sphere floating beside him. Around the rim of the door were antigravity beamers and heavy duty stun guns. The opposite side of the sphere wasn't there; it simply faded away.

To Svotz that was the most frightening thing about any time machine: the way it seemed to turn a corner that wasn't there.

Svetz was almost over the signal. Now he used the remote controls to swing the antigravity beamers around and down.

He had them locked on the source. He switched them on, and dials surged.

Leviathan was *heavy.* More massive than Svetz had expected. Svetz upped the power, and watched the NAI needle swing as Leviathan rose invisibly through the water.

Where the surface of the water bulged upward under the attack of the antigravity beams, a shadow formed. Leviathan rising . . .

Was there something wrong with the shape?

Then a trembling spherical bubble of water rose shivering from the ocean, and Leviathan was within it.

Partly within it. He was too big to fit, though he should not have been.

He was four times as massive as a sperm whale should have been, and a dozen times as long. He looked nothing like the crystal Steuben sculpture. Leviathan was a kind of serpent armored with red-bronze scales as big as a Viking's shield, armed with teeth like ivory spears. His triangular jaws gaped wide. As he floated toward Svetz he writhed, seeking with his bulging yellow eyes for whatever strange enemy had subjected him to this indignity.

Svetz was paralyzed with fear and indecision. Neither then nor later did he doubt that what he saw was the Biblical Leviathan. This had to be the largest beast that had ever roamed the sea; a beast large enough and fierce enough to be synonymous with anything big and destructive. Yet—if the crystal sculpture was anything like representational, this was not a sperm whale at all.

In any case, he was far too big for the extension cage. Indecision stayed his hand—and then Svetz stopped thinking entirely, as the great slitted irises found him.

The beast was floating past him. Around its waist was a sphere of weightless water, that shrank steadily as gobbets dripped away and rained back to the sea. The beast's nostrils flared—it was obviously an air-breather, though not a cetacean.

It stretched, reaching for Svetz with gaping jaws.

Teeth like scores of elephant's tusks all in a row. Polished and needle sharp. Svetz saw them close about him from above and below, while he sat frozen in fear.

At the last moment he shut his eyes tight.

When death did not come, Svetz opened his eyes.

The jaws had not entirely closed on Svetz and his armchair. Svetz heard them grinding faintly against—against the invisible surface of the extension cage, whose existence Svetz had forgotten entirely.

Svetz resumed breathing. He would return home with an empty extension cage, to face the wrath of Ra Chen . . . a fate better than death. Svetz moved his fingers to cut the antigravity beams from the big extension cage.

Metal whined against metal. Svetz whiffed hot oil, while red lights bloomed all over his lunch-tray control board. He hastily turned the beams on again.

The red lights blinked out one by reluctant one.

Through the transparent shell Svetz could hear the grinding of teeth. Leviathan was trying to chew his way into the extension cage.

His released weight had nearly torn the cage loose from the rest of the time machine. Svetz would have been stranded in the past, a hundred miles out to sea, in a broken extension cage that probably wouldn't float, with an angry sea monster waiting to snap him up. No, he couldn't turn off the antigravity beamers.

But the beamers were on the big extension cage, and he couldn't keep the big extension cage more than about fifteen minutes longer. When the big extension cage was gone, what would prevent Leviathan from pulling him to his doom?

"I'll stun him off," said Svetz.

There was dark red palate above him, and red gums and forking tongue beneath, and the long curved fangs all around. But between the two rows of teeth Svetz could see the big extension cage, and the battery of stunners around the door. By eye he rotated the stunners until they pointed straight toward Leviathan.

"I must be out of my mind," said Svetz, and he spun the stunners away from him. He couldn't fire the stunners at Leviathan without hitting himself.

And Leviathan wouldn't let go.

Trapped.

No, he thought with a burst of relief. He could escape with his life. The go-home lever would send his small extension cage out from between the jaws of Leviathan, back into the time stream, back to the Institute. His mission had failed, but that was hardly his fault. Why had Ra Chen been unable to uncover mention of a sea serpent bigger than a sperm whale?

"It's all his fault," said Svetz. And he reached for the go-home lever. But he stayed his hand.

"I can't just tell him so," he said. For Ra Chen terrified him.

The grinding of teeth came itchingly through the extension cage.

"Hate to just quit," said Svetz. "Think I'll try something . . ."

He could see the antigravity beamers by looking between the teeth. He could feel their influence, so nearly were they focussed on the extension cage itself. If he focussed them just on himself . . .

He felt the change; he felt both strong and light-headed, like a drunken ballet master. And if he now narrowed the focus . . .

27

The monster's teeth seemed to grind harder. Svetz looked between them as best he could.

Leviathan was no longer floating. He was hanging straight down from the extension cage, hanging by his teeth. The antigravity beamers still balanced the pull of his mass; but now they did so by pulling straight up on the extension cage.

The monster was in obvious distress. Naturally. A water beast, he was supporting his own mass for the first time in his life. And by his teeth! His yellow eyes rolled frantically. His tail twitched slightly at the very tip. And still he clung . . .

"Let go," said Svetz. "Let go, you . . . monster."

The monster's teeth slid screeching down the transparent surface, and he fell.

Svetz cut the antigravity a fraction of a second late. He smelled burnt oil, and there were tiny red lights blinking off one by one on his lunch-tray control board.

Leviathan hit the water with a sound of thunder. His long, sinuous body rolled over and floated to the surface and lay as if dead. But his tail flicked once, and Svetz knew that he was alive.

"I could kill you," said Svetz. "Hold the stunners on you until you're dead. There's time enough . . ."

But he still had ten minutes to search for a sperm whale. It wasn't time enough. It didn't begin to be time enough, but if he used it all . . .

The sea serpent flicked its tail and began to swim away. Once he rolled to look at Svetz, and his jaws opened wide in fury. He finished his roll and was fleeing again.

"Just a minute," Svetz said thickly. "Just a science-perverting minute there . . ." And he swung the stunners to focus.

Gravity behaved strangely inside an extension cage. While the cage was moving forward in time, *down* was all directions outward from the center of the cage. Svetz was plastered against the curved wall. He waited for the trip to end.

Seasickness was nothing compared to the motion sickness of time travel.

Free fall, then normal gravity. Svetz moved unsteadily to the door.

Ra Chen was waiting to help him out. "Did you get it?"

"Leviathan? No sir." Svetz looked past his boss. "Where's the big extension cage?"

"We're bringing it back slowly, to minimize the gravitational side effects. But if you don't have the whale—"

"I said I don't have Leviathan."

"Well, just what *do* you have?" Ra Chen demanded.

Somewhat later he said, "It wasn't?"

Later yet he said, "You killed him? Why, Svetz? Pure spite?"

"No, sir. It was the most intelligent thing I did during the entire trip."

"But *why?* Never mind, Svetz, here's the big extension cage." A grey-blue shadow congealed in the hollow cradle of the time machine. "And there does seem to be something in it. Hi, you idiots, throw an antigravity beam inside the cage! Do you want the beast crushed?"

The cage had arrived. Ra Chen waved an arm in signal. The door opened.

Something tremendous hovered within the big extension cage. It looked like a malevolent white mountain in there, peering back at its captors with a single tiny, angry eye. It was trying to get at Ra Chen, but it couldn't swim in air.

Its other eye was only a torn socket. One of its flippers was ripped along the trailing edge. Rips and ridges and puckers of scar tissue, and a forest of broken wood and broken steel, marked its tremendous expanse of albino skin. Lines trailed from many of the broken harpoons. High up on one flank, bound to the beast by broken and tangled lines, was the corpse of a bearded man with one leg.

"Hardly in mint condition, is he?" Ra Chen observed.

"Be careful, sir. He's a killer. I saw him ram a sailing ship and sink it clean before I could focus the stunners on him."

"What amazes me is that you found him at all in the time you had left. Svetz, I do not understand your luck. Or am I missing something?"

"It wasn't luck, sir. It was the most intelligent thing I did the entire trip."

"You said that before. About killing Leviathan."

Svetz hurried to explain. "The sea serpent was just leaving the vicinity. I wanted to kill him, but I knew I didn't have the time. I was about to leave myself, when he turned back and bared his teeth.

"He was an obvious carnivore. Those teeth were built strictly for killing, sir. I should have noticed earlier. And I could think of only one animal big enough to feed a carnivore that size."

"Ah-h-h. Brilliant, Svetz."

"There was corroborative evidence. Our research never found any mention of giant sea serpents. The great geological surveys of the first century Post Atomic should have turned up something. Why didn't they?"

"Because the sea serpent quietly died out two centuries earlier, after whalers killed off his food supply."

Svetz colored. "Exactly. So I turned the stunners on Leviathan before he could swim away, and I kept the stunners on him until the NAI said he was dead. I reasoned that if Leviathan was here, there must be whales in the vicinity."

"And Leviathan's nervous output was masking the signal."

"Sure enough, it was. The moment he was dead the NAI registered another signal. I followed it to—" Svetz jerked his head. They were floating the whale out of the extension cage. "To him."

Days later, two men stood on one side of a thick glass wall.

"We took some clones from him, then passed him on to the Secretary-General's vivarium," said Ra Chen. "Pity you had to settle for an albino." He waved aside Svetz's protest: "I know, I know, you were pressed for time."

Beyond the glass, the one-eyed whale glared at Svetz through murky seawater. Surgeons had removed most of the harpoons, but scars remained along his flanks; and Svetz, awed, wondered how long the beast had been at war with Man. Centuries? How long did sperm whales live?

Ra Chen lowered his voice. "We'd all be in trouble if the Secretary-General found out that there was once a bigger animal than his. You understand that, don't you, Svetz?"

"Yes sir."

"Good." Ra Chen's gaze swept across another glass wall, and a fire-breathing Gila monster. Further down, a horse looked back at him along the dangerous spiral horn in its forehead.

"Always we find the unexpected," said Ra Chen. "Sometimes I wonder . . ."

If you'd do your research better, Svetz thought . . .

"Did you know that time travel wasn't even a concept until the first century Ante Atomic? A writer invented it. From then until the fourth century Post Atomic, time travel was pure fantasy. It violates everything the scientists of the time thought were natural laws. Logic. Conservation of matter and energy. Momentum, reaction, any law of motion that makes time a part of the statement. Relativity.

"It strikes me," said Ra Chen, "that every time we push

an extension cage past that particular four-century period, we shove it into a kind of fantasy world. That's why you keep finding giant sea serpents and fire breathing—"

"That's nonsense," said Svetz. He was afraid of his boss, yes; but there were limits.

"You're right," Ra Chen said instantly. Almost with relief. "Take a month's vacation, Svetz, then back to work. The Secretary-General wants a bird."

"A bird?" Svetz smiled. A bird sounded harmless enough. "I suppose he found it in another children's book?"

"That's right. Ever hear of a bird called a *roc?*"

BIRD IN THE HAND

"It's not a roc," said Ra Chen.

The bird looked stupidly back at them from behind a thick glass wall. Its wings were small and underdeveloped; its legs and feet were tremendous, ludicrous. It weighed three hundred pounds and stood nearly eight feet tall.

Other than that, it looked a lot like a baby chick.

"It kicked me," Svetz complained. A slender, small boned man, he stood stiffly this day, with a slight list to port. "It kicked me in the side and broke four ribs. I barely made it back to the extension cage."

"It still isn't a roc. Sorry about that, Svetz. We did some research in the history section of the Beverly Hills Library while you were in the hospital. The roc was only a legend."

"But look at it!"

Svetz's beefy, red faced boss nodded. "That's probably what started the legend. Early explorers in Australia saw these—*ostriches* wandering about. They said to themselves, 'If the chicks are this size, what are the adults like?' Then they went home and told stories about the adults."

"I got my ribs caved in for a flightless bird?"

"Cheer up, Svetz. It's not a total loss. The ostrich was extinct. It makes a fine addition to the Secretary-General's vivarium."

"But the Secretary-General wanted a roc. What are you going to tell him?"

Ra Chen scowled. "It's worse than that. Do you know what the Secretary-General wants now?"

People meeting Ra Chen for the first time thought he was constantly scowling, until they saw his *scowl.* Svetz had suspected Ra Chen was worried. Now he knew it.

The Secretary-General was everybody's problem. A recessive gene inherited from his powerful, inbred family had left him with the intelligence of a six-year-old child. Another kind of inheritance had made him overlord of the Earth and its colonies. His whim was law throughout the explored universe.

Whatever the Secretary-General wanted now, it was vital that he get it.

"Some idiot took him diving in Los Angeles," Ra Chen said. "He wants to see the city before it sank."

"That doesn't sound too bad."

"It wouldn't be, if it had stopped there. Some of his Circle of Advisors noticed his interest. They got him historical tapes on Los Angeles. He loves them. He wants to join the first Watts Riot."

Svetz gulped. "That should raise some security problems."

"You'd think so, wouldn't you? The Secretary-General is almost pure caucasian."

The ostrich cocked its head to one side, studying them. It still looked like the tremendous chick of an even bigger bird. Svetz could imagine that it had just cracked its way out of an egg the size of a bungalow.

"I'm going to have a headache," he said. "Why do you tell me these things? You *know* I don't like politics."

"Can you imagine what would happen if the Secretary-General got himself killed with the help of the Institute for Temporal Research? There are enough factions already that would like to see us disbanded. Space, for instance; they'd *love* to swallow us up."

"But what can we do? We can't turn down a direct request from the Secretary-General!"

"We can distract him."

They had lowered their voices to conspiratorial whispers. Now they turned away from the ostrich and strolled casually down the line of glass cages.

"How?"

"I don't know yet. If I could only get to his nurse," Ra Chen said between his teeth. "I've tried hard enough. Maybe the Institute for Space Research has bought her. Then again, maybe she's loyal. She's been with him thirty-four years.

"How do I know what would catch his attention? I've only met the Secretary-General four times, all on formal occasions. But his attention span is low. He'd forget about Los Angeles if we could distract him."

The cage they were passing was labeled:

ELEPHANT
Retrieved from the year 700 AnteAtomic, approximately, from the region of India, Earth, EXTINCT.

The wrinkled grey beast watched them go with sleepy indifference. His air of inhuman age and wisdom was such that he must have recognized Svetz as his captor. But he didn't care.

Svetz had captured almost half of the animals in the Vivarium. And Svetz was afraid of animals. Especially big animals. Why did Ra Chen keep sending him after animals?

The thirty feet of lizard in the next cage (*GILA MONSTER*, the placard said) definitely recognized Svetz. It jetted orange-white flame at him, and flapped its tiny batlike wings in fury when the flame washed harmlessly across the glass. If it ever got loose—

But that was why the cages were airtight. The animals of Earth's past must be protected from the air of Earth's present.

Svetz remembered the cobalt-blue sky of Earth's past

35

and was reassured. Today's afternoon sky was brilliant turquoise at the zenith, shading through pastel green and yellow to rich yellow-brown near the horizon. If the Chinese fire-breather ever got out, it would be too busy gasping for purer air to attack Svetz.

"What can we get him? I think he's tired of these animals. Svetz, what about a giraffe?"

"A what?"

"Or a dog, or a satyr . . . it's got to be unusual," Ra Chen muttered. "A teddy bear?"

Out of his fear of animals, Svetz ventured, "I wonder if you might not be on the wrong track, sir."

"Mph? Why?"

"The Secretary-General has enough animals to satisfy a thousand men. Worse than that, you're competing with Space when you bring back funny animals. They can do that too."

Ra Chen scratched behind his ear. "I never thought of that. You're right. But we've got to do *something*."

"There must be lots of things to do with a time machine."

They could have taken a displacement plate back to the Center. Ra Chen preferred to walk. It would give him a chance to think, he said.

Svetz walked with bowed head and blind eyes alongside his boss. Inspiration had come to him at similar times. But they had reached the red sandstone cube that was the Center, and the mental lightning had not struck.

A big hand closed on his upper arm. "Just a minute," Ra Chen said softly. "The Secretary-General's paying us a visit."

Svetz's heart lurched. "How do you know?"

"You should recognize that machine in the walkway. We brought it back last month from Los Angeles, from the day of the Great California Earthquake. It's an internal combustion automobile. It belongs to the Secretary-General."

"What'll we do?"

"Go in and show him around. Pray he doesn't insist on being taken back to Watts, August eleventh, twenty Post Atomic."

"Suppose he does?" If they boiled Ra Chen for treason, they would surely boil Svetz too.

"I'll have to send him back if he asks it. Oh, not with you, Svetz. With Zeera. She's black, and she speaks american. It might help."

"Not enough," said Svetz, but he was already calmer. Let Zeera take the risks.

They passed close by the Secretary-General's automobile. Svetz was intrigued by its odd, angular look, its complex control panels, the shiny chrome trim. Someone had removed the hood, so that the polished complexity of the motor was open to view.

"Wait," Svetz said suddenly. "Does he like it?"

"*Will* you come on?"

"Does the Secretary-General like his automobile?"

"Sure, Svetz. He loves it."

"Get him another car. California must have been full of automobiles on the day before the Great Quake."

Ra Chen stopped suddenly. "That could be it. It would hold him for awhile, give us time . . ."

"Time for what?"

Ra Chen didn't hear. "A racing car . . .? No, he'd kill himself. The Circle of Advisors would want to install a robot chauffeur-override. Maybe a dune buggy?"

"Why not ask *him*?"

"It's worth a try," said Ra Chen. They went up the steps.

In the Center there were three time machines, including the one with the big extension cage, plus a host of panels with flashing colored lights. The Secretary-General liked those. He smiled and chuckled as Ra Chen led him about. His guards hovered at his shoulders, their faces stiff, their fingernails clicking against their gunbutts.

Ra Chen introduced Svetz as "my best agent." Svetz was so overwhelmed by the honor that he could only stutter. But the Secretary-General didn't seem to notice.

Whether he had forgotten about seeing the Watts Riot was moot; but he did forget to ask on that occasion.

When Ra Chen asked about cars, the Secretary-General smiled all across his face and nodded so vigorously that Svetz worried about spinal injury. Faced by a vast array of choices, five or six decades with dozens of new models for every year, the Secretary-General put his finger in his mouth and considered well.

Then he made his choice.

" 'Why not ask him? Why not ask him?' " Ra Chen mimicked savagely. "Now we know. The first car! He wants the first car ever made!"

"I thought he'd ask for a *make* of car." Svetz rubbed his eyes hard. "How can we possibly find one car? A couple of decades to search through, and all of the North American and European continents!"

"It's not that bad. We'll use the books from the Beverly Hills Library. But it's bad enough, Svetz . . ."

The raid on the Beverly Hills Library had been launched in full daylight, using the big extension cage and a dozen guards armed with stunners, on June third, twenty-six PostAtomic. Giant time machines, crazy men wearing flying belts—on any other day it would have made every newspaper and television program in the country. But June the third was a kind of Happy Hunting Ground for the Institute for Temporal Research.

No Californian would report the raid, except to other Californians. If the story did get out, it would be swamped by more important news. The series of quakes would begin at sunset, and the ocean would rise like a great green wall . . .

Svetz and Ra Chen and Zeera Southworth spent half the night going through the history section of the Beverly Hills Library. Ra Chen knew enough white american to recognize titles; but in the end Zeera had to do all the reading.

Zeera Southworth was tall and slender and very dark, crowned with hair like a black powder explosion. She sat gracefully cross-legged on the floor, looking very angular, reading pertinent sections aloud while the others paced. They followed a twisting trail of references.

By two in the morning they were damp and furious.

"Nobody invented the automobile!" Ra Chen exploded. "It just happened!"

"We certainly have a wide range of choices," Zeera agreed. "I take it we won't want any of the steam automobiles. That would eliminate Gugnot and Trevethick and the later British steam coaches."

"We'll concentrate on internal combustion."

Svetz said, "Our best bets seem to be Lenoir of France and Marcus of Vienna. Except that Daimler and Benz have good claims, and Selden's patent held good in court—"

"Dammit, pick one!"

"Just a minute, sir." Zeera alone retained some semblance of calm. "This Ford might be the best we've got."

"Ford? Why? He invented nothing but a system of mass production."

Zeera held up the book. Svetz recognized it: a biography she had been reading earlier. "This book implies that Ford was responsible for everything: that he created the automobile industry singlehanded."

"But we know that isn't true," Svetz protested.

Ra Chen made a pushing motion with one hand. "Let's not be hasty. We take Ford's car, and we produce that book to authenticate it. Who'll know the difference?"

"But if someone does the same research we just—oh. Sure. He'll get the same answers. No answers. Ford's just as good a choice as anyone else."

"Better, if nobody looks further," Zeera said with satisfaction. "Too bad we can't take the Model T; it looks much more like an automobile. This thing he started with looks like a kiddy cart. It says he built it out of old pipes."

"Tough," said Ra Chen.

Late the next morning, Ra Chen delivered last-minute instructions.

"You can't just take the car," he told Zeera. "If you're interrupted, come back without it."

"Yes, sir. It would be less crucial if we took our duplicate from a later time, from the Smithsonian Institution, for instance."

"The automobile has to be new. Be reasonable, Zeera! We can't give the Secretary-General a second-hand automobile!"

"No sir."

"We'll land you about three in the morning. Use infrared and pills to change your vision. Don't show any visible light. Artificial light would probably scare them silly."

"Right."

"Were you shown—"

"I know how to use the duplicator." Zeera sounded faintly supercilious, as always. "I also know that it reverses the image."

"Never mind that. Bring back the reversed duplicate, and we'll just reverse it again."

"Of course." She seemed chagrined that she had not seen that for herself. "What about dialect?"

"You speak black and white american, but it's for a later period. Don't use slang. Stick to black unless you want to impress someone white. Then speak white, but speak slowly and carefully and use simple words. They'll think you're from another country. I hope."

Zeera nodded crisply. She stooped and entered the extension cage, turned and pulled the duplicator after her. Its bulk was small, but it weighed a ton or so without the lift field generator to float it. One end glowed white with glow-paint.

They watched the extension cage blur and vanish. It was still attached to the rest of the time machine, but attached along a direction that did not transmit light.

"Now then!" Ra Chen rubbed his hands together. "I don't expect she'll have any trouble getting Henry Ford's flightless flight stick. Our trouble may come when the Secretary-General sees what he's got."

Svetz nodded, remembering the grey-and-flat pictures in the history books. Ford's machine was ungainly, slipshod, ugly and undependable. A few small surreptitious additions would make it dependable enough to suit the Secretary-General. *Nothing* would make it beautiful.

"We need another distraction," said Ra Chen. "We've only bought ourselves more time to get it."

Zeera's small time machine gave off a sound of ripping cloth, subdued, monotonous, reassuring. A dozen workmen were readying the big extension cage. Zeera would need it to transport the duplicate automobile.

"There's something I'd like to try," Svetz ventured.

"Concerning what?"

"The roc."

Ra Chen grinned. "The ostrich? Svetz, don't you ever give up?"

Svetz looked stubborn. "Do you know anything about neoteny?"

"Never heard of it. Look, Svetz, we're going to be over budget because of the roc trip. Not your fault, of course, but another trip would cost us over a million commercials."

"I won't need the time machine."

"Oh?"

"But I could use the help of the Palace Veterinarian. Have you got enough pull to arrange that?"

The Palace Veterinarian was a stocky, blocky, busty woman with muscular legs and a thrusting jaw. A floating platform packed with equipment followed her between the rows of cages.

"I know most of these beasts," she told Svetz. "Once upon a time I was going to give them all names. An animal ought to have a name."

"They've got names."

"That's what I decided. *GILA MONSTER, ELEPHANT, OSTRICH*," she read. "You give Horace a name so you won't mix him up with Gilbert. But nobody would get *HORSE* mixed up with *ELEPHANT*. There's only one of each. Poor beasties." She stopped before the cage marked *OSTRICH*. "Is this your prize? I've been meaning to come see him."

The bird shifted its feet in indecision; it cocked its head to consider the couple on the other side of the glass. It seemed surprised at Svetz's return.

"He looks just like a newly hatched chick," she said. "Except for the legs and feet, of course. They seem to have developed to support the extra mass."

Svetz was edgy with the need to be in two places at once. His own suggestion had sparked Zeera's project. He ought to be at the Center. Yet—the ostrich had been his first failure.

He asked, "Does it look neotenous?"

"Neotenous? Of course. Neoteny is a common method of evolution. We have neotenous traits ourselves, you know. Bare skin, where all the other primates are covered with hair. When our ancestors started chasing their meat across the plains, they needed a better cooling system than most primates need. So they kept one aspect of immaturity, the bare skin. Probably the big head is another one.

"The axolotl is the classic example of neoteny—"

"Excuse me?"

"You know what a salamander was, don't you? It had gills and fins while immature. As an adult it grew lungs and shed the gills and lived on land. The axolotl was a viable offshoot that never lost the gills and fins. A gene shift, typical of neoteny."

"I never heard of either of them, axolotls or salamanders."

"They needed open streams and ponds to live, Svetz."

Svetz nodded. If they needed open water, then both species must be over a thousand years extinct.

"The problem is that we don't know when your bird lost its ability to fly. Some random neotenous development may have occurred far in the past, so that the bird's wings never developed. Then it may have evolved its present size to compensate."

"Oh. Then the ancestor—"

"May have been no bigger than a turkey. Shall we go in and find out?"

The glass irised open to admit them. Svetz stepped into the cage, felt the tug of the pressure curtain flowing over and around him. The ostrich backed warily away.

The vet opened a pouch on her floating platform, withdrew a stunner, and used it. The ostrich squawked in outrage and collapsed. No muss, no fuss.

The vet strode toward her patient—and stopped suddenly in the middle of the cage. She sniffed, sniffed again in horror. "Have I lost my sense of smell?"

Svetz produced two items like cellophane bags, handed her one. "Put this on."

"Why?"

"You might suffocate if you don't." He donned the other himself, by pulling it over his head, then pressing the rim against the skin of his neck. It stuck. When he finished he had a hermetic seal.

"This air is deadly," he explained. "It's the air of the Earth's past, reconstituted. Think of it as coming from fifteen hundred years ago. There's no civilization. Nothing's been burned yet. That's why you can't smell anything but ostrich.

"Out there— Well, you don't really need sulphur dioxide and carbon monoxide and nitric oxides to stay alive. You do need carbon dioxide. There's a nerve complex in the lymph glands under your left armpit, and it triggers the breathing reflex. It's activated by a certain concentration of CO_2 in the blood."

She had finished donning her filter helmet. "I take it the concentration is too low in here."

"Right. You'd forget to breathe. You're used to air that's four percent carbon dioxide. In here it's barely a tenth of that.

"The bird can breathe this bland stuff. In fact, it'd die without it. What we've put into the air in the past fifteen hundred years, we've had fifteen hundred years to adapt to. The ostrich hasn't."

"I'll keep that in mind," she said shortly; so that Svetz wondered if he'd been lecturing someone who knew more than he did. She knelt beside the sleeping ostrich, and the platform floated lower for her convenience.

Svetz watched her as she ministered to the ostrich, taking tissue samples, testing blood pressure and heartbeat in reaction to small doses of hormones and drugs.

In a general way he knew what she was doing. There were techniques for reversing the most recent mutations in an animal's genetic makeup. One did not always get what one expected. Still—there was a *homo habilis* several cages down, who had been in the Circle of Advisors until he called the Secretary-General a tyrannical fugghead.

While she was identifying the neotenous developments, she would also be trying to guess what she would have when they were eliminated. Then there were matters of metabolism. If Svetz was right, the bird's mass would increase rapidly. It must be fed intravenously, and even more rapidly.

In general—but the details of what she was doing were mysterious and dull.

Svetz found himself studying her filter helmet. Full inflation had rendered it almost invisible. A golden rim of it showed by diffraction against the yellow-brown sky.

Did Space really want to take over the Institute for Temporal Research? Then that golden halo was support for their claim. It was a semipermeable membrane. It would selectively pass gasses in both directions in such a way as to make an almost breathable atmosphere breathable.

It had been taken unchanged from a Space warehouse.

Other ITR equipment had come from the space industries. Flight sticks. Anaesthetic needle guns. The low mass antigravity unit in the new extension cage.

But their basic argument was more subtle.

Once the ocean teemed with life, Svetz thought. *Now the continental shelf is as dead as the Moon: nothing but bubble cities. Once this whole continent was all forest and living desert and fresh water. We cut down the trees and shot the animals and poisoned the rivers and irrigated the deserts so that even the desert life died; and now there's nothing left but the food yeast and us.*

We've forgotten so much about the past that we can't separate legend from fact. We've wiped out most of the forms of life on Earth in the last fifteen hundred years,

45

*and changed the composition of the air to the extent that
we'd be afraid to change it back.*

*I fear the unknown beasts of the past. I cannot breathe
the air. I do not know the edible plants. I could not kill
the animals for food. I do not know which would kill me.*

*The Earth's past is as alien to me as another planet.
Let Space have it!*

The Palace Veterinarian was busy jabbing the pointed
ends of color-coded tubing into various portions of the
bird's anatomy. The tubes led back to machinery on the
floating platform.

Svetz's pocket phone rang. He flipped it open.

"There's trouble," said Ra Chen's image. "Zeera's cage
is on its way home. She must have pulled the go-home
lever right after she called for the big extension cage."

"She left before the big cage could get there?"

Ra Chen nodded grimly. "Whatever happened must
have happened fast. If she called for the big cage,
then she had the automobile. A moment later she aborted
the mission. Svetz, I'm worried."

"I'd hate to leave now, sir." Svetz turned to look at the
ostrich. In that moment all of the bird's feathers fell out,
leaving it plump and naked.

That decided him. "I can't leave now, sir. We'll have
a full-grown roc here in another ten minutes."

"What? *Good!* But how?"

"The ostrich was a neotenous offshoot of the roc. We've
produced a throwback."

"Good! Stick with it, Svetz. We'll handle it here." Ra
Chen switched off.

The Palace Veterinarian said, "You shouldn't make
promises you can't keep."

Svetz's heart leapt. "Trouble?"

"No. It's going beautifully so far."

46

"All the feathers fell out. Is that good?"

"Don't worry about it. See for yourself: already there's a coat of down. Your ostrich is reverting to chickhood," she said cheerfully. "Its ancestor's chickhood. If the ancestor really was no bigger than a turkey before it lost the ability to fly, it'll be even smaller as a chick."

"What'll happen then?"

"It'll drown in its own fat."

"We should have taken a clone."

"Too late. Look at it now: look at the legs. They aren't nearly as overdeveloped."

The bird was a big ball of pale yellow down. Its frame had shrunk, but its legs had shrunk much more. Standing, it would have been no more than four feet tall. The extra mass had turned to fat, so that the ostrich was nearly spherical; it bulged like a poolside toy, lying on its inflated side in a pool of feathers.

"Now it *really* looks like a chick," said Svetz.

"It does, Svetz. In fact, it is. That was a *big* chick. The adult is going to be tremendous." The Palace Veterinarian jumped to her feet. "Svetz, we've got to hurry. Is there a basic dole yeast source in this cage?"

"Sure. Why?"

"He'll starve at the rate he's growing, unless . . . Just show me, Svetz."

The animals of the Zoo ate dole yeast, like everyone else, but with special additives for each animal. A brain tap could induce the animal to imagine it was eating whatever it was used to eating when the time probe had picked it up.

Svetz showed her the yeast tap. She hooked the pipeline to one of the machines on her floating platform; she made adaptations, added another machine . . . .

The bird grew visibly. Its fat layer shrank, deflated. Its legs and wings stretched outward. The beak began to take a distinctive hooked form, sharp and wicked.

Svetz began to feel panic. Beneath its downy feathers the bird was little more than taut skin stretched over long bones.

The yeast was now feeding directly into two tanks on the floating platform, and from there into the colored tubes. Somehow the Palace Veterinarian was converting the yeast directly into sugar-plasma.

"It's working now," she said. "I wasn't sure it would. He'll be all right now, if the growth cycle slows down in time." She smiled up at him. "You were right all along. The ostrich was a neotenous roc."

At that moment the light changed.

Svetz wasn't sure what had disturbed him. But he looked up—and the sky was baby blue from the horizon to the zenith.

"What is it?" The woman beside him was bemused rather than frightened. "I never saw a color like that in my life!"

"I have."

"What is it?"

"Don't worry about it. But keep your filter helmet on, especially if you have to leave the cage. Can you remember that?"

"Of course." Her eyes narrowed. "You know something about this, Svetz. It's something to do with time, isn't it?"

"I think so." Svetz used the key beam then, to avoid further questions. The glass peeled back to let him out.

He turned for a last look through the glass.

The Palace Veterinarian looked frightened. She must have guessed too much for her own comfort. But she turned away to care for her patient.

The ostrich lay on its side, its eyes open now. It was

tremendous, and still scrawny despite the volume of the intravenous feed. Its feathers were changing color. The bird would be black and green.

It was half as big as the elephant next door . . . whose air of grey wisdom was giving way to uneasiness as he watched the proceedings.

It looked nothing like an ostrich.

The sky was baby blue, the blue of the deep past, crossed with fluffy clouds of clean and shining white. Blue from the horizon to the zenith, without a trace of the additives that ought to be there.

Unconscious men and women lay everywhere. Svetz dared not stop to help. What he had to do was more important.

He slowed to a walk as he neared the Center. There was pain like a knife blade inserted between his partly healed ribs.

ITR crewmen had fallen in the walkway around the Center, presumably after staggering outside. And there was the Secretary-General's automobile sitting quietly in front. Behind it, flat on his back, was Ra Chen.

What did he think he was doing there?

Svetz heard the purr of the motor as he approached. So that was it. Ra Chen must have hoped that the exhaust would revive him. Damn clever; and it should have worked. Why hadn't it?

Svetz looked into the polished metal guts of the motor as he passed. The motor had changed . . . somehow. What ran it now? Steam? Electricity? A flywheel? In any event, the exhaust pipe Ra Chen had been searching for was no longer there.

Ra Chen was alive, his pulse rapid and frantic. But he wasn't breathing. Or . . . yes, he was. He was breathing perhaps twice a minute as carbon dioxide built up enough to activate the reflex.

Svetz went on into the Center.

More than a dozen men and women had collapsed across lighted control panels. Three more figures sprawled in an aisle. The Secretary-General lay in angular disorder, smiling foolishly up at the ceiling. His guards wore troubled sleeping expressions and held drawn guns.

The small extension cage had not returned.

Svetz looked into the empty gap in the time machine, and felt terror. What could he accomplish without Zeera to tell him what had gone wrong?

From 50 Ante Atomic to the present was a thirty minute trip. Ra Chen's call to the Zoo must have come less than thirty minutes ago. Weird, how an emergency could telescope time.

Unless that was a side effect of the paradox. Unless the paradox had chopped away Zeera's extension cage and left her stranded in the past, or cast off into an alternate world line, or . . .

There had never been a temporal paradox.

Math was no help. The mathematics of time travel was riddled with singularities.

Last year somebody had tried to do a topological analysis of the path of an extension cage. He had proved not only that time travel was impossible, but that you couldn't travel faster than light either. Ra Chen had leaked the news to Space on the off chance that their hyperdrive ships would stop working.

What to do? Start putting filter helmets on everyone? Great, but the helmets weren't kept at the Center; he'd have to go across town. Did he dare leave the Center?

Svetz forced himself to sit down.

Minutes later, he snapped alert at the *pop* of displaced air. The small extension cage had returned. Zeera was crawling out of the circular doorway.

"Get back in there," Svetz ordered. "Quick!"

"I don't take orders from you, Svetz." She brushed past him and looked about her. "The automobile's gone. Where's Ra Chen?" Zeera's face was blank with shock and exhaustion. Her voice was a monotone, ragged at the edges.

Svetz took her arm. "Zeera, we've—"

She jerked away. "We've got to *do* something. The automobile's gone. Didn't you hear me?"

"Did you hear *me?* Get back in the extension cage!"

"But we've got to decide what to *do*. Why can't I smell anything?" She sniffed at air that was scentless, empty, dead. She looked about her in bewilderment, realizing for the first time just how strange everything was.

Then the eyes rolled up in her head, and Svetz stepped forward to catch her.

He studied her sleeping face across the diameter of the extension cage. It was very different from her waking face. Softer, more vulnerable. And prettier. Zeera had quite a pretty face.

"You should relax more often," he said.

His ribs throbbed where the ostrich had kicked him. The pain seemed to beat like a heart.

Zeera opened her eyes. She asked, "Why are we in here?"

"The extension cage has its own air system," said Svetz. "You can't breathe the outside air."

"Why not?"

"You tell me."

Her eyes went wide. "The automobile! It's gone!"

"Why?"

"I don't know. Svetz, I *swear* I did everything right. But when I turned on the duplicator the automobile disappeared!"

"That . . . doesn't sound at all good." Svetz strove to keep his voice level. "What did you—"

"I did it just the way they taught me! I hooked the glow painted end to the frame, set the dials for an estimated mass plus a margin of error, read the dials off—"

"You must have hooked up the wrong end somehow. Wait a minute. Were you using the infrared flash?"

"Of course. It was dead of night."

"And you'd taken the pills so you'd be able to see infrared."

"Do you always think that slowly, Svetz?" Then her eyes changed. "I was seeing infrared. Of course. I hooked up the *hot* end."

"The duplicator end. That would duplicate empty space where there was an automobile. You'd get emptiness at both ends."

"Stupid," Zeera said bitterly. "Stupid."

She hooked her arms under her knees and relaxed against the curved side of the extension cage. Presently she said, "Henry Ford sold that automobile for two hundred dollars, according to the book. Later he had trouble getting financed."

"How much is two hundred dollars?"

"I think it depends on the year. Enough to ruin a man, apparently, if you take it away at the right time. Then someone else used assembly lines to make automobiles. And he must have liked steam or electricity."

"Steam, I'd guess. Steam cars came first."

"Why would that affect the air? We can breathe what comes out of an automobile exhaust pipe, but we don't need it to live. Except CO_2. A steam automobile would burn fuel, wouldn't it?"

"I wondered about that too," said Svetz. "It took me awhile, but I got it. Some of what comes out of an exhaust pipe never goes away. It just stays in the air, like a curtain between us and the sun. It's been there for a thousand years, cutting off half our sunlight. And we made it didn't happen."

"Photosynthesis. *That's* where all the carbon dioxide went."

"Right."

"But if the air changed, why didn't we change with it? We evolved to be able to breathe a certain kind of air. Shouldn't the evolution have been cancelled too? For that matter, why do we remember?"

"I don't know. There's a lot we don't know about time travel."

"I'm not nagging, Svetz. I don't know either."

More silence.

"It's clear enough," Zeera said presently. "I'll have to go back and warn myself to get the duplicator on straight."

"That won't work. It *didn't* work. If you'd gotten the ends of the duplicator on straight we wouldn't be *in* this mess. Therefore you didn't."

"Logic and time travel don't go, remember?"

"Maybe we can go *around* you." Svetz hesitated, then plunged in. "Try this. Send me back to an hour before the earlier Zeera arrives. The automobile won't have disappeared yet. I'll duplicate it, duplicate the duplicate, take the reversed duplicate and the original past you in the big extension cage. That leaves you to destroy the duplicate. I reappear after you're gone, leave the original automobile for Ford, and come back here with the reverse duplicate. How's that?"

"It sounded great. Would you mind going through it again?"

"Let's see. I go back to—"

She was laughing at him. "Never mind. But it has to be me, Svetz. You couldn't find your way. You couldn't ask directions or read the street signs. You'll have to stay here and man the machinery."

Svetz was crawling out of the extension cage when there came a scream like the end of the world.

Momentarily he froze. Then he dashed around the swelling flank of the cage. Zeera followed, wearing the filter helmet she had worn during her attempt to duplicate Ford's automobile.

One wall of the Center was glass. It framed a crest of hill across from the palace, and a double row of cages that made up the Zoo. One of the cages was breaking apart as they watched, smashing itself to pieces like—

—Like an egg hatching. And like a chick emerging, the roc stood up in the ruin of its cage.

The scream came again.

"What is it?" Zeera whispered.

"It was an ostrich. I'd hate to give it a name now."

The bird seemed to move in slow motion. There was so much of it! Green and black, beautiful and evil, big as eternity, and a crest of golden feathers had sprouted on its forehead. Its hooked beak descended toward a cage.

That cage ripped like tissue paper.

Zeera was shaking his arm. "Come on! If it came from the Zoo, we don't need to worry about it. It'll suffocate when we get the car back where it belongs."

"Oh. Right," said Svetz. They went to work moving the big extension cage a few hours further back in time.

When Svetz looked again, the bird was just taking to the air. Its wings flapped like sails, and their black shadows swept like clouds over the houses. As the roc rose fully into view, Svetz saw that something writhed and struggled in its tremendous talons.

Svetz recognized it . . . and realized just how big the roc really was.

"It's got *ELEPHANT*," he said. An inexplicable sorrow gripped his heart. Inexplicable, for Svetz hated animals.

"What? Come *on*, Svetz!"

"Um? Oh, yes." He helped Zeera into the small extension cage and sent it on its way.

Despite its sleeping crew, the machinery of the Center

was working perfectly. If anything got off, Svetz would have six men's work to do. Therefore he prowled among the control boards, alert for any discrepancy, making minor adjustments . . . And occasionally he looked out the picture window.

The roc had reached an enormous height. Any other bird would have been invisible long since. But the roc was all too apparent, hovering in the blue alien sky while it killed and ate *ELEPHANT*.

Bloody bones fell in the walkway.

Time passed.

Twenty minutes for Zeera to get back.

More time to make two duplicates of the automobile. Load them into the big extension cage. Then to signal Svetz—

The signal came. She had the cars. Svetz played it safe, moved her forward six hours, almost to dawn on the crucial night. She might be caught by an early riser, but at least Ford would have his automobile back.

The roc had finished its bloody meal. *ELEPHANT* was gone. And—Svetz watched until he was sure—the bird was dropping, riding down the sky on outstretched wings.

Svetz watched it grow bigger, and bigger yet, until it seemed to enfold the universe. It settled over the Center like a tornado cloud, in darkness, and wind. Like twin tornado funnels, two sets of curved talons touched down in the walkway.

The bird bent low. An inhuman face looked in at Svetz through the picture window. It nearly filled the window.

It knows me, Svetz thought. *Even a bird's brain must be intelligent in a head that size.*

The vast head rose out of sight above the roof.

I had the ostrich. I should have been satisfied, thought Svetz. *A coin in the hand is worth two in the street.* The ancient proverb could as easily be applied to birds.

The roof exploded downward around a tremendous hooked beak. Particles of concrete spattered against walls and floor. A yellow eye rolled and found Svetz, but the beak couldn't reach him. Not through *that* hole.

The head withdrew through the roof.

Three red lights. Svetz leapt for the board and began twisting dials. He made two lights turn green, then the third. It had not occurred to him to run. The bird would find him out wherever he hid . . .

There! Zeera had pulled the go-home lever. From here it was all automatic.

Crash!

Svetz was backed up against the big time machine, pinned by a yellow eye as big as himself. Half the roof was gone now. Still the curved beak couldn't reach him. But a great claw came seeking him through the shattered glass.

The light changed.

Svetz sagged. Behind the green and black feathers he could see that the sky had turned pale yellow-green, marked with yellow-brown streamers of cloud.

The bird sniffed incredulously, once, twice. Somehow the panic showed in its tremendous eye, before the great head rose through the roof. The roc stepped back from the Center for clearance; its dark wings swept down like night falling.

Svetz was beyond fear or common sense. He stepped out to watch it rise.

He had to hug an ornamental pillar. The wind of the wings was a hurricane. The bird looked down once, and recognized him, and looked away.

It was still well in view, rising and circling, when Zeera stepped out to join him. Presently Ra Chen was there to follow their eyes. Then half the Center maintenance team was gaping up in awe and astonishment.

The bird dwindled to a black shadow. Black against pastel green, climbing, climbing.

Suffocating.

One sniff had been enough. The bird's brain was as enormously proportioned as the rest of it. It had started climbing immediately, without waiting to snatch up Svetz for its dessert.

Climbing, climbing toward the edge of space. Reaching for clean air.

The Secretary-General stood beside Svetz, smiling in wonder, chuckling happily as he gazed upward.

Was the roc still climbing? No, the black shadow was growing larger, sliding down the sky. And the slow motion of the wings had stopped.

How was a roc to know that there was no clean air anywhere?

THERE'S A WOLF
IN MY TIME MACHINE

The old extension cage had no fine controls; but that hardly mattered. It wasn't as if Svetz were chasing some particular extinct animal. Ra Chen had told him to take whatever came to hand.

Svetz guided the cage back to pre-industrial America, somewhere in mid-continent, around 1000 Ante Atomic Era. Few humans, many animals. Perhaps he'd find a bison.

And when he pulled himself to the window, he looked out upon a vast white land.

Svetz had not planned to arrive in mid-winter.

Briefly he considered moving into the time stream again and using the interrupter circuit. Try another date, try luck again. But the interrupter circuit was new, untried, and Svetz wasn't about to be the first man to test it.

Besides which, a trip into the past cost over a million commercials. Using the interrupter circuit would nearly double that. Ra Chen would be displeased.

Svetz began freezing to death the moment he opened the door. From the doorway the view was all white, with one white bounding shape far away.

Svetz shot it with a crystal of soluble anaesthetic.

He used the flight stick to reach the spot. Now that it was no longer moving, the beast was hard to find. It was just the color of the snow, but for its open red mouth and the black pads on its feet. Svetz tentatively identified it as an arctic wolf.

It would fit the Vivarium well enough. Svetz would

have settled for anything that would let him leave this frozen wilderness. He felt uncommonly pleased with himself. A quick, easy mission.

Inside the cage, he rolled the sleeping beast into what might have been a clear plastic bag, and sealed it. He strapped the wolf against one curved wall of the extension cage. He relaxed into the curve of the opposite wall as the cage surged in a direction vertical to all directions.

Gravity shifted oddly.

A transparent sac covered Svetz's own head. Its lip was fixed to the skin of his neck. Now Svetz pulled it loose and dropped it. The air system was on; he would not need the filter sac.

The wolf would. It could not breathe industrial age air. Without the filter sac to remove the poisons, the wolf would choke to death. Wolves were extinct in Svetz's time.

Outside, time passed at a furious rate. Inside, time crawled. Nestled in the spherical curve of the extension cage, Svetz stared up at the wolf, who now seemed fitted into the curve of the ceiling.

Svetz had never met a wolf in the flesh. He had seen pictures in children's books . . . and even the children's books had been stolen from the deep past. Why should the wolf look so familiar?

It was a big beast, possibly as big as Hanville Svetz, who was a slender, small-boned man. Its sides heaved with its panting. Its tongue was long and red and its teeth were white and sharp.

Like the dogs, Svetz remembered. The dogs in the Vivarium, in the glass case labeled:

DOG
CONTEMPORARY

Alone of the beasts in the Vivarium, the dogs were not sealed in glass for their own protection. The others could not breathe the air outside. The dogs could.

In a very real sense, they were the work of one man. Lawrence Wash Porter had lived near the end of the Industrial Period, between 50 and 100 Post Atomic Era, when billions of human beings were dying of lung diseases while scant millions adapted. Porter had decided to save the dogs.

Why the dogs? His motives were obscure, but his methods smacked of genius. He had acquired members of each of the breeds of dog in the world, and bred them together, over many generations of dogs and most of his own lifetime.

There would never be another dog show. Not a purebred dog was left in the world. But hybrid vigor had produced a new breed. These, the ultimate mongrels, could breathe industrial age air, rich in oxides of carbon and nitrogen, scented with raw gasoline and sulfuric acid.

The dogs were behind glass because people were afraid of them. Too many species had died. The people of 1100 Post Atomic were not used to animals.

Wolves and dogs . . . could one have sired the other?

Svetz looked up at the sleeping wolf and wondered. He was both like and unlike the dogs. The dogs had grinned out through the glass and wagged their tails when children waved. Dogs liked people. But the wolf, even in sleep . . .

Svetz shuddered. Of all the things he hated about his profession, this was the worst: the ride home, staring up at a strange and extinct animal. The first time he'd done it, a captured horse had seriously damaged the control panel. On his last mission an ostrich had kicked him and broken three ribs.

The wolf was stirring restlessly . . . and something about it had changed.

Something was changing now. The beast's snout was shorter, wasn't it? Its forelegs lengthened peculiarly; its paws seemed to grow and spread. Svetz caught his breath.

Svetz caught his breath, and instantly forgot the wolf.

Svetz was choking, dying. He snatched up his filter sac and threw himself at the controls.

Svetz stumbled out of the extension cage, took three steps and collapsed. Behind him, invisible contaminants poured into the open air.

The sun was setting in banks of orange cloud.

Svetz lay where he had fallen, retching, fighting for air. There was an outdoor carpet beneath him, green and damp, smelling of plants. Svetz did not recognize the smell, did not at once realize that the carpet was alive. He would not have cared at that point. He knew only that the cage's air system had tried to kill him. The way he felt, it had probably succeeded.

It had been a near thing. He had been passing 30 Post Atomic when the air went bad. He remembered clutching the interrupter switch, then waiting, waiting. The foul air stank in his nostrils and caught in his throat and tore at his larynx. He had waited through twenty years, feeling every second of them. At 50 Post Atomic he had pulled the interrupter switch and run choking from the cage.

50 PA. At least he had reached industrial times. He could breathe the air.

It was the horse, he thought without surprise. The horse had pushed its wickedly pointed horn through Svetz's control panel, three years ago. Maintenance was supposed to fix it. They *had* fixed it.

Something must have worn through.

The way he looked at me every time I passed his cage. I always knew the horse would get me, Svetz thought.

He noticed the filter sac still in his hand. Not that he'd be—

Svetz sat up suddenly.

There was green all about him. The damp green carpet beneath him was alive; it grew from the black ground.

A rough, twisted pillar thrust from the ground, branched into an explosion of red and yellow papery things. More of the crumpled colored paper lay about the pillar's base. Something that was not an aircraft moved erratically overhead, a tiny thing that fluttered and warbled.

Living, all of it. A pre-industrial wilderness.

Svetz pulled the filter sac over his head and hurriedly smoothed the edges around his neck to form a seal. Blind luck that he hadn't fainted yet. He waited for it to puff up around his head. A selectively permeable membrane, it would pass the right gasses in and out until the composition of the air was—was—

Svetz was choking, tearing at the sac.

He wadded it up and threw it, sobbing. First the air plant, now the filter sac! Had someone wrecked them both? The inertial calendar too; he was at least a hundred years previous to 50 Post Atomic.

Someone had tried to kill him.

Svetz looked wildly about him. Uphill across a wide green carpet, he saw an angular vertical-sided formation painted in shades of faded green. It had to be artificial. There might be people there. He could—

No, he couldn't ask for help either. Who would believe him? How could they help him anyway? His only hope was the extension cage. And his time must be very short.

The extension cage rested a few yards away, the door a black circle on one curved side. The other side seemed to fade away into nothing. It was still attached to the rest of the time machine, in 1103 PA, along a direction eyes could not follow.

Svetz hesitated near the door. His only hope was to disable the air plant somehow. Hold his breath, then—

The smell of contaminants was gone.

Svetz sniffed at the air. Yes, gone. The air plant had exhausted itself, drained its contaminants into the open air. No need to wreck it now. Svetz was sick with relief.

He climbed in.

He remembered the wolf when he saw the filter sac, torn and empty. Then he saw the intruder towering over him, the coarse thick hair, the yellow eyes glaring, the taloned hands spread wide to kill.

The land was dark. In the east a few stars showed, though the west was still deep red. Perfumes tinged the air. A full moon was rising.

Svetz staggered uphill, bleeding.

The house on the hill was big and old. Big as a city block, and two floors high. It sprawled out in all directions, as though a mad architect had built to a whim that changed moment by moment. There were wrought iron railings on the upper windows, and wrought iron handles on the screens on both floors, all painted the same dusty shade of green. The screens were wood, painted a different shade of green. They were closed across every window. No light leaked through anywhere.

The door was built for someone twelve feet tall. The knob was huge. Svetz used both hands and put all his weight into it, and still it would not turn. He moaned. He looked for the lens of a peeper camera and could not find it. How would anyone know he was here? He couldn't find a doorbell either.

Perhaps there was nobody inside. No telling what this building was. It was far too big to be a family dwelling, too spread out to be a hotel or apartment house. Might it be a warehouse or a factory? Making or storing what?

Svetz looked back toward the extension cage. Dimly he caught the glow of the interior lights. He also saw something moving on the living green that carpeted the hill.

Pale forms, more than one.

Moving this way?

Svetz pounded on the door with his fists. Nothing. He

noticed a golden metal thing, very ornate, high on the door. He touched it, pulled at it, let it go. It clanked.

He took it in both hands and slammed the knob against its base again and again. Rhythmic clanking sounds. Someone should hear it.

Something zipped past his ear and hit the door hard. Svetz spun around, eyes wild, and dodged a rock the size of his fist. The white shapes were nearer now. Bipeds, walking hunched.

They looked too human—or not human enough.

The door opened.

She was young, perhaps sixteen. Her skin was very pale, and her hair and brows were pure white, quite beautiful. Her garment covered her from neck to ankles, but left her arms bare. She seemed sleepy and angry as she pulled the door open—manually, and it was heavy, too. Then she saw Svetz.

"Help me," said Svetz.

Her eyes went wide. Her ears moved too. She said something Svetz had trouble interpreting, for she spoke in ancient american.

"What *are* you?"

Svetz couldn't blame her. Even in good condition his clothes would not fit the period. But his blouse was ripped to the navel, and so was his skin. Four vertical parallel lines of blood ran down his face and chest.

Zeera had been coaching him in the american speech. Now he said carefully, "I am a traveler. An animal, a monster, has taken my vehicle away from me."

Evidently the sense came through. "You poor man! What kind of animal?"

"Like a man, but hairy all over, with a horrible face—and claws—claws—"

"I see the mark they made."

"I don't know how he got in. I—" Svetz shuddered. No, he couldn't tell her that. It was insane, utterly insane, this conviction that Svetz's wolf had become a bloodthirsty humanoid monster. "He only hit me once. On the face. I could get him out with a weapon, I think. Have you a bazooka?"

"What a funny word! I don't think so. Come inside. Did the trolls bother you?" She took his arm and pulled him in and shut the door.

Trolls?

"You're a strange person," the girl said, looking him over. "You look strange, you smell strange, you move strangely. I did not know that there were people like you in the world. You must come from very far away."

"Very," said Svetz. He felt himself close to collapse. He was safe at last, safe inside. But why were the hairs on the back of his neck trying to stand upright?

He said, "My name is Svetz. What's yours?"

"Wrona." She smiled up at him, not afraid despite his strangeness . . . and he must look strange to her, for she surely looked strange to Hanville Svetz. Her skin was sheet white, and her rich white hair would better have fit a centenarian. Her nose, very broad and flat, would have disfigured an ordinary girl. Somehow it fit Wrona's face well enough; but her face was most odd, and her ears were too large, almost pointed, and her eyes were too far apart, and her grin stretched *way* back . . . and Svetz liked it. Her grin was curiosity and enjoyment, and was not a bit too wide. The firm pressure of her hand was friendly, reassuring. Though her fingernails were uncomfortably long and sharp.

"You should rest, Svetz," she said. "My parents will not be up for another hour, at least. Then they can decide how to help you. Come with me, I'll take you to a spare room."

He followed her through a room dominated by a great rectangular table and a double row of high-backed chairs. There was a large microwave oven at one end, and beside it a platter of . . . red things. Roughly conical they were, each about the size of a strong man's upper arm, each with a dot of white in the big end. Svetz had no idea what they were; but he didn't like their color. They seemed to be bleeding.

"Oh," Wrona exclaimed. "I should have asked. Are you hungry?"

Svetz was, suddenly. "Have you dole yeast?"

"Why, I don't know the word. Are those dole yeast? They are all we have."

"We'd better forget it." Svetz's stomach lurched at the thought of eating something that color. Even if it turned out to be a plant.

Wrona was half supporting him by the time they reached the room. It was rectangular and luxuriously large. The bed was wide enough, but only six inches off the floor, and without coverings. She helped him down to it. "There's a wash basin behind that door, if you find the strength. Best you rest, Svetz. In perhaps two hours I will call you."

Svetz eased himself back. The room seemed to rotate. He heard her go out.

How strange she was. How odd he must look to her. A good thing she hadn't called anyone to tend him. A doctor would notice the differences.

Svetz had never dreamed that primitives would be so different from his own people. During the thousand years between now and the present, there must have been massive adaptation to changes in air and water, to DDT and other compounds in foods, to extinction of food plants and meat animals until only dole yeast was left, to higher noise levels, less room for exercise, greater dependence on medicines . . . Well, why shouldn't they be different? It was a wonder humanity had survived at all.

Wrona had not feared his strangeness, nor cringed from the scratches on his face and chest. She was only amused and interested. She had helped him without asking too many questions. He liked her for that.

He dozed.

Pain from deep scratches, stickiness in his clothes made his sleep restless. There were nightmares. Something big and shadowy, half man and half beast, reached far out to slash his face. Over and over. At some indeterminate time he woke completely, already trying to identify a musky, unfamiliar scent.

No use. He looked about him, at a strange room that seemed even stranger from floor level. High ceiling. One frosted globe, no brighter than a full moon, glowed so faintly that the room was all shadow. Wrought iron bars across the windows; black night beyond.

A wonder he'd wakened at all. The pre-industrial air should have killed him hours ago.

It had been a futz of a day, he thought. And he shied from the memory of the thing in the extension cage. The snarling face, pointed ears, double row of pointed white teeth. The clawed hand reaching out, swiping down. The nightmare conviction that a wolf had turned into *that*.

It could not be. Animals did not change shape like that. Something must have gotten in while Svetz was fighting for air. Chased the wolf out, or killed it.

But there were legends of such things, weren't there? Two and three thousand years old and more, everywhere in the world, were the tales of men who could become beasts and vice versa.

Svetz sat up. Pain gripped his chest, then relaxed. He stood up carefully and made his way to the bathroom.

The spiggots were not hard to solve. Svetz wet a cloth with warm water. He watched himself in the mirror, emerging from under the crusted blood. A pale, slender young man topped with thin blond hair . . . and an odd distortion of chin and forehead. That must be the mirror, he decided. Primitive workmanship. It might have been worse. Hadn't the first mirrors been two-dimensional?

A shrill whistle sounded outside his door. Svetz went to look, and found Wrona. "Good, you're up," she said. "Father and Uncle Wrocky would like to see you."

Svetz stepped into the hall, and again noticed the elusive musky scent. He followed Wrona down the dark hall way. Like his room, it was lit only by a single white frosted globe. Why would Wrona's people keep the house so dark? They had electricity.

And why were they all sleeping at sunset? With breakfast laid out and waiting . . .

Wrona opened a door, gestured him in.

Svetz hesitated a step beyond the threshold. The room was as dark as the hallway. The musky scent was stronger here. He jumped when a hand closed on his upper arm—it felt wrong, there was hair on the palm, the hard nails made a circlet of pressure points—and a gravelly male voice boomed, "Come in, Mister Svetz. My daughter tells me you're a traveler in need of help."

In the dim light Svetz made out a man and a woman seated on backless chairs. Both had hair as white as Wrona's, but the woman's hair bore a broad black stripe. A second man urged Svetz toward another backless chair. He too bore black markings: a single black eyebrow, a black crescent around one ear.

And Wrona was just behind him. Svetz looked around at them all, seeing how like they were, how different from Hanville Svetz.

The fear rose up in him like a strong drug. Svetz was a xenophobe.

They were all alike. Rich white hair and eyebrows, black markings. Narrow black fingernails. The broad flat noses and the wide, wide mouths, the sharp white conical teeth, the high, pointed ears that moved, the yellow eyes, the hairy palms.

Svetz dropped heavily onto the padded footstool.

One of the males noticed: the larger one, who was still standing. "It must be the heavier gravity," he guessed. "It's true, isn't it, Svetz? You're from another world. Obviously you're not quite a man. You told Wrona you were a traveler, but you didn't say from how far away."

69

"Very far," Svetz said weakly. "From the future."

The smaller male was jolted "The future? You're a time traveler?" His voice became a snarl. "You're saying that we will evolve into something like you!"

Svetz cringed. "No. Really."

"I hope not. What, then?"

"I think I must have gone sidewise in time. You're descended from wolves, aren't you? Not apes. Wolves."

"Yes, of course."

The seated male was looking him over. "Now that he mentions it, he does look much more like a troll than any man has a right to. No offense intended, Svetz."

Svetz, surrounded by wolf men, tried to relax. And failed. "What is a troll?"

Wrona perched on the edge of his stool. "You must have seen them on the lawn. We keep about thirty."

"Plains apes," the smaller male supplied. "Imported from Africa, sometime in the last century. They make good watchbeasts and meat animals. You have to be careful with them, though. They throw things."

"Introductions," the other said suddenly. "Excuse our manners, Svetz. I'm Flakee Wrocky. This is my brother Flakee Worrel, and Brenda, his wife. My niece you know."

"Pleased to meet you," Svetz said hollowly.

"You say you slipped sideways in time?"

"I think so. A futz of a long way, too," said Svetz. "Marooned. Gods protect me. It must have been the horse—"

Wrocky broke in. "Horse?"

"The horse. Three years ago, a horse damaged my extension cage. It was supposed to be fixed. I suppose the repairs just wore through, and the cage slipped sideways in time instead of forward. Into a world where wolves evolved instead of *Homo habilis.* Gods know where I'm likely to wind up if I try to go back."

Then he remembered. "At least you can help me

there. Some kind of monster has taken over my extension cage."

"Extension cage?"

"The part of the time machine that does the moving. You'll help me evict the monster?"

"Of course," said Worrel, at the same time the other was saying, "I don't think so. Bear with me, please, Worrel. Svetz, it would be a disservice to you if we chased the monster out of your extension cage. You would try to reach your own time, would you not?"

"Futz, yes!"

"But you would only get more and more lost. At least in our world you can eat the food and breathe the air. Yes, we grow food plants for the trolls; you can learn to eat them."

"You don't understand. I can't stay here. I'm a xeno-phobe!"

Wrocky frowned. His ears flicked forward enquiringly. "What?"

"I'm afraid of intelligent beings who aren't human. I can't help it. It's in my bones."

"Oh, I'm sure you'll get used to us, Svetz."

Svetz looked from one male to the other. It was obvious enough who was in charge. Wrocky's voice was much louder and deeper than Worrel's; he was bigger than the other man, and his white fur fell about his neck in a mane like a lion's. Worrel was making no attempt to assert himself. As for the women, neither had spoken a word since Svetz entered the room.

Wrocky was emphatically the boss. And Wrocky didn't want Svetz to leave.

"You don't understand," Svetz said desperately. "The air—" He stopped.

"What about the air?"

"It should have killed me by now. A dozen times over. In fact, why hasn't it?" Odd enough that he'd ever stopped wondering about that. "I must have adapted," Svetz said half to himself. "That's it. The cage passed too close to this line of history. My heredity changed. My lungs adapted to pre-industrial air. Futz it! If I hadn't pulled the interrupter switch I'd have adapted back!"

"Then you can breathe our air," said Wrocky.

"I still don't understand it. Don't you have any industries?"

"Of course," Worrel said in surprise.

"Internal combustion cars and aircraft? Diesel trucks and ships? Chemical fertilizers, insect repellents—"

"No, none of that. Chemical fertilizers wash away, ruin the water. The only insect repellents I ever heard of smelled to high heaven. They never got beyond the experimental stage. Most of our vehicles are battery powered."

"There *was* a fad for internal combustion once," said Wrocky. "It didn't spread very far. They stank. The people inside didn't care, of course, because they were leaving the stink behind. At its peak there were over two hundred cars tootling around the city of Detroit, poisoning the air. Then one night the citizenry rose in a pack and tore all the cars to pieces. The owners too."

Worrel said, "I've always thought that men have more sensitive noses than trolls."

"Wrona noticed my smell long before I noticed hers. Wrocky, this is getting us nowhere. I've *got* to go home. I seem to have adapted to the air, but there are other things. Foods: I've never eaten anything but dole yeast; everything else died out long ago. Bacteria."

Wrocky shook his head. "Anywhere you go, Svetz, your broken time machine will only take you to more and more exotic environments. There must be a thousand ways the world could end. Suppose you stepped out into one of them? Or just passed near one?"

"But—"

"Here, on the other paw, you will be an honored guest.

Think of all the things you can teach us! You, who were born into a culture that builds time traveling vehicles!"

So that was it. "Oh, no. You couldn't use what I know," said Svetz. "I'm no mechanic. I couldn't show you how to do anything. Besides, you'd hate the side effects. Too much of past civilizations was built on petrochemicals. And plastics. Burning plastics produces some of the strangest—"

"But even the most extensive oil reserves could not last forever. You must have developed other power sources by your own time." Wrocky's yellow eyes seemed to bore right through him. "Controlled hydrogen fusion?"

"But I can't tell you how it's done!" Svetz cried desperately. "I know nothing of plasma physics!"

"Plasma physics? What are plasma physics?"

"Using electromagnetic fields to manipulate ionized gasses. You *must* have plasma physics."

"No, but I'm sure you can give us some valuable hints. Already we have fusion bombs. And so do the Europeans . . . but we can discuss that later." Wrocky stood up. His black nails made pressure points on Svetz's arm. "Think it over, Svetz. Oh, and make yourself free of the house, but don't go outside without an escort. The trolls, you know."

Svetz left the room with his head whirling. The wolves would not let him leave.

"Svetz, I'm glad you're staying," Wrona chattered. "I like you. I'm sure you'll like it here. Let me show you the house."

Down the length of the hallway, one frosted globe burned dimly in the gloom, like a full moon transported indoors. Nocturnal, they were nocturnal.

Wolves.

"I'm a xenophobe," he said. "I can't help it. I was born that way."

"Oh, you'll learn to like us. You like me a little already, don't you, Svetz?" She reached up to scratch him behind the ear. A thrill of pleasure ran through him, unexpectedly sharp, so that he half closed his eyes.

"This way," she said.

"Where are we going?"

"I thought I'd show you some trolls. Svetz, are you really descended from trolls? I can't believe it!"

"I'll tell you when I see them," said Svetz. He remembered the *Homo habilis* in the Vivarium. It had been a man, an Advisor, until the Secretary-General ordered him regressed.

They went through the dining room, and Svetz saw unmistakable bones on the plates. He shivered. His forebears had eaten meat; the trolls were brute animals here, whatever they might be in Svetz's world—but Svetz shuddered. His thinking seemed turgid, his head felt thick. He had to get out of here.

"If you think Uncle Wrocky's tough, you should meet the European ambassador," said Wrona. "Perhaps you will."

"Does he come here?"

"Sometimes." Wrona growled low in her throat. "I don't like him. He's a different species, Svetz. Here it was the wolves that evolved into men; at least that's what our teacher tells us. In Europe it was something else."

"I don't think Uncle Wrocky will let me meet him. Or even tell him about me." Svetz rubbed at his eyes.

"You're lucky. Herr Dracula smiles a lot and says nasty things in a polite voice. It takes you a minute to— Svetz! What's wrong?"

Svetz groaned like a man in agony. "My eyes!" He felt higher. "My forehead! I don't have a forehead any more!"

"I don't understand."

Svetz felt his face with his fingertips. His eyebrows were a caterpillar of hair on a thick, solid ridge of bone.

From the brow ridge his forehead sloped back at forty-five degrees. And his chin, his chin was gone too. There was only a regular curve of jaw into neck.

"I'm regressing. I'm turning into a troll," said Svetz. "Wrona, if I turn into a troll, will they eat me?"

"I don't know. I'll stop them, Svetz!"

"No. Take me down to the extension cage. If you're not with me the trolls will kill me."

"All right. But, Svetz, what about the monster?"

"He should be easier to handle by now. It'll be all right. Just take me there. Please."

"All right, Svetz." She took his hand and led him.

The mirror hadn't lied. He'd been changing even then, adapting to this line of history. First his lungs had lost their adaptation to normal air. There had been no industrial age here. But there had been no Homo sapiens either . . .

Wrona opened the door. Svetz sniffed at the night. His sense of smell had become preternaturally acute. He smelled the trolls before he saw them, coming uphill toward him across the living green carpet. Svetz's fingers curled, wishing for a weapon.

Three of them. They formed a ring around Svetz and Wrona. One of them carried a length of white bone. They all walked upright on two legs, but they walked as if their feet hurt them. They were as hairless as men. Apes' heads mounted on men's bodies.

Homo habilis, the killer plains ape. Man's ancestor.

"Pay them no attention," Wrona said offhandedly. "They won't hurt us." She started down the hill. Svetz followed closely.

"He really shouldn't have that bone," she called back. "We try to keep bones away from them. They use them as weapons. Sometimes they hurt each other. Once one of them got hold of the iron handle for the lawn sprinkler and killed a gardener with it."

"I'm not going to take it away from him."

"That glaring light, is that your extension cage?"

"Yes."

"I'm not sure about this, Svetz." She stopped suddenly. "Uncle Wrocky's right. You'll only get more lost. Here you'll at least be taken care of."

"No. Uncle Wrocky was wrong. See the dark side of the extension cage, how it fades away to nothing? It's still attached to the rest of the time machine. It'll just reel me in."

"Oh."

"No telling how long it's been veering across the time lines. Maybe ever since that futzy horse poked his futzy horn through the controls. Nobody ever noticed before. Why should they? Nobody ever stopped a time machine halfway before."

"Svetz, horses don't have horns."

"Mine does."

There was noise behind them. Wrona looked back into a darkness Svetz's eyes could not pierce. "Somebody must have noticed us! Come on, Svetz!"

She pulled him toward the lighted cage. They stopped just outside.

"My head feels thick," Svetz mumbled. "My tongue too."

"What are we going to do about the monster? I can't hear anything—"

"No monster. Just a man with amnesia, now. He was only dangerous in the transition stage."

She looked in. "Why, you're right! Sir, would you mind —Svetz, he doesn't seem to understand me."

"Sure not. Why should he? He thinks he's a white arctic wolf." Sevtz stepped inside. The white haired wolf man was backed into a corner, warily watching. He looked a lot like Wrona.

Svetz became aware that he had picked up a tree branch. His hand must have done it without telling his brain. He circled, holding the weapon ready. An unreasoning rage built up and up in him. Invader! The man had no business here in Svetz's territory.

The wolf man backed away, his slant eyes mad and frightened. Suddenly he was out the door and running, the trolls close behind.

"Your father can teach him, maybe," said Svetz.

Wrona was studying the controls. "How do you work it?"

"Let me see. I'm not sure I remember." Svetz rubbed at his drastically sloping forehead. "That one closes the door—"

Wrona pushed it. The door closed.

"Shouldn't you be outside?"

"I want to come with you," said Wrona.

"Oh." It was getting terribly difficult to think. Svetz looked over the control panel. Eeny, meeny,—that one? Svetz pulled it.

Free fall. Wrona yipped. Gravity came, vectored radially outward from the center of the extension cage. It pulled them against the walls.

"When my lungs go back to normal, I'll probably go to sleep," said Svetz. "Don't worry about it." Was there something else he ought to tell Wrona? He tried to remember.

Oh, yes. "You can't go home again," said Svetz. "We'd never find this line of history again."

"I want to stay with you," said Wrona.

"All right."

Within a deep recess in the bulk of the time machine, a fog formed. It congealed abruptly—and Svetz's extension cage was back, hours late. The door popped open automatically. But Svetz didn't come out.

They had to pull him out by the shoulders, out of air that smelled of beast and honeysuckle.

"He'll be all right in a minute. Get a filter tent over

that other thing," Ra Chen ordered. He stood over Svetz with his arms folded, waiting.

Svetz began breathing.

He opened his eyes.

"All right," said Ra Chen. "What happened?"

Svetz sat up. "Let me think. I went back to pre-industrial America. It was all snowed in. I . . . shot a wolf."

"We've got it in a tent. Then what?"

"No. The wolf left. We chased him out." Svetz's eyes went wide. "Wrona!"

Wrona lay on her side in the filter tent. Her fur was thick and rich, white with black markings. She was built something like a wolf, but more compactly, with a big head and a short muzzle and a tightly curled tail. Her eyes were closed. She did not seem to be breathing.

Svetz knelt. "Help me get her out of there! Can't you tell the difference between a wolf and a dog?"

"No. Why would you bring back a dog, Svetz? We've got dozens of dogs."

Svetz wasn't listening. He pulled away the filter tent and bent over Wrona. "I think she's a dog. More dog than wolf, anyway. People tend to domesticate each other. She's adapted to our line of history. And our brand of air." Svetz looked up at his boss. "Sir, we'll have to junk the old extension cage. It's been veering sideways in time."

"Have you been eating gunchy pills on the job?"

"I'll tell you all about it—"

Wrona opened her eyes. She looked about her in rising panic until she found Svetz. She looked up at him, her golden eyes questioning.

"I'll take care of you. Don't worry," Svetz told her. He scratched her behind the ear, his fingertips deep in soft fur. To Ra Chen he said, "The Vivarium doesn't need any more dogs. She can stay with me."

"Are you crazy, Svetz? You, live with an animal? You hate animals!"

"She saved my life. I won't let anyone put her in a cage."

"Sure, keep it! Live with it! I don't suppose you plan to pay back the two million commercials she cost us? I thought not." Ra Chen made a disgusted sound. "All right, let's have your report. And keep that thing under control, will you?"

Wrona raised her nose and sniffed at the air. Then she howled. The sound echoed within the Institute, and heads turned in questioning and fear.

Puzzled, Svetz imitated the gesture, and understood.

The air was rich with petrochemicals and oxides of carbon and nitrogen and sulfur. Industrial air, the air Svetz had breathed all his life.

And Svetz hated it.

DEATH IN A CAGE

Svetz was coming home.

His narrow arms were folded on his chest. His back curved like a bow, to fit him into the curvature of the extension cage. He lay motionless, in stoic endurance, watching the inertial calendar.

Gravity behaved oddly in an extension cage. The pull was outward now as the cage moved into the future. —41, —40 . . . Svetz could not have reached the controls without considerable effort. They were overhead, at the center of the spherical shell. He did not need to reach them. The bulk of the time machine was fixed in time/space at the Institute for Temporal Research in 1102 Post Atomic. It would simply reel him in.

The small armored thing he'd captured was strapped to an opposite wall. It had not moved since Svetz shot it with an anaesthetic crystal.

The numbers on the inertial calendar rolled upward. +16, +17, +18 . . . Gravity jumped and shivered like a car on a bumpy road. Svetz lay on his back and tried to ignore what his belly and his inner ear were telling him. In a couple of hours, internal time, he'd be home.

Something smoky began to obscure the control panel.

Svetz sniffed. The air was thick with oxides of nitrogen and sulfur, carbon monoxide and carbon dioxide and carbon tetrachloride, a mixture of industrial wastes that Svetz had been breathing since the day he was born. He sniffed and found nothing unusual.

81

But the haze was thickening.

It was not fanning out. It hung before the control panel, taking shape.

Svetz rubbed his eyes. It was still there, a shape like a cloaked and hooded man, distorting colors and outlines where they showed through. A vague stick-figure hand moulded itself around a lever, and pulled.

The interrupter circuit!

Svetz sat up. His head swam. He tried to stand, and overbalanced, and fell rolling.

The apparition braced its smoky feet against the control panel, heedless of the switches and dials. Its feet and ankles were terribly thin. It pantomimed frantic effort . . . but the lever marked EMERGENCY STOP did not move.

The figure turned to Svetz and screamed at him without sound. Svetz screamed back and threw his arms across his eyes. That face!

When Svetz dared look again, the thing was gone.

Svetz began to shake. The inertial calendar read +36, +37 . . .

"Ghosts, eh?" Svetz's beefy, red faced boss scowled ferociously. At least he was taking it seriously. He might as easily have sent Svetz off for a psychiatric examination. "That's all we need. A haunted time machine. Well, have you got any idea what really happened?"

"There must be something wrong with the time machine. I think we ought to give up using it until we find out what."

"You do."

"Yes sir."

"Come here a minute." Ra Chen took Svetz's arm and walked away with him. He was twice Svetz's mass; his hand wrapped one and a half times around Svetz's bicep.

He stopped them before the picture window that fronted the Institute for Temporal Research.

Spread below them, the shops and houses and crooked streets of the city of Capitol. On the hill across the valley, tremendous and daunting, the complex of buildings that was the United Nations Palace.

Ra Chen pointed downhill. "There."

There was a gap in the cityscape. A cluster of broken houses surrounded the broken corpse of a bird, a bird the size of a five story building. It had been there for two weeks now. The stink reached them even here.

"Our worst failure to date. I forebear to point out to you, Svetz, that it was your idea to use regression treatments on an ostrich. Notice, however, that the futzy thing lies in full view of the Palace. We'll have to do something spectacular before the Advisors forget that gaff! And we'd better do it soon."

"Yes sir."

"We're in bad odor at the Palace, Svetz."

"Sir, I think that's the roc."

Ra Chen glared.

"We're already missing one time machine," he continued. "I had to yank it after we found out it was veering sidewise in time, across probability lines. The technical arm is still trying to find something wrong with it. Now you want me to yank the other one. Svetz, could you have imagined this—manifestation?"

"I've asked myself that."

"Well?"

"No, sir. It was real. Even if I could see through it."

"It's just such a lousy time to lose both time machines. Appropriations come up in three months."

The vets were removing his armadillo from the extension cage. Svetz watched them erect a gauzy filter tent over it to protect it from the air of 1102 Post Atomic.

"We ought to give up on funny animals," said Ra

Chen. "The Secretary-General already has more extinct animals than he knows what to do with. We ought to try something else."

"Yes, sir. But what?"

Ra Chen didn't answer. They watched as the medical team took clone samples from the armadillo, then moved away with it. It was awake, but doing very little to prove it. Tomorrow it would be in the Vivarium.

"This ghost, now," Ra Chen said suddenly. "Was it human, or just humanoid?"

"It—there was something wrong with the face. Something dreadful."

"But was it a man or an alien?"

"I couldn't tell. After all, it was thin as smoke! It was wearing a robe. I couldn't see anything but the face and hands—and they were dreadfully thin. It looked like a walking skeleton."

"A skeleton, huh? Maybe you were seeing through the flesh. Like a holo of a man in X-ray light."

"That sounds right."

"But why? Why would he be transparent?"

"Funny, I was just wondering the same thing."

"Don't be sarcastic, Svetz."

"Sorry, sir."

"We've both been assuming it was a sign of something wrong with the time machine. What if it wasn't? What if the thing was real?"

Svetz shook his head violently. "There are no such things as ghosts."

"We thought that about rocs. Why not? Think how long the ghost legend has been around. All over the world, in burial customs, folk tales, all the great religions. There are people who believe in ghosts even today. Not many, I admit—"

"But, sir, it's nonsense! Even if there were real ghosts, what*ever* they are, how would they get aboard an extension cage? And what could we do about it?"

"Capture it, of course. The Secretary-General would love it. He could even play with it; it sounded harmless enough—"

"But!"

"—Just ugly. As for how it got there, how should I know? I don't know anything about the theory of time travel. It should be possible to duplicate the conditions—"

"You say it's harmless. I saw it. I say it isn't!"

"We can look into that after we've got it. Svetz, we need a *coup*. We're going after that ghost."

"We? Me! And I won't!"

"Come," said Ra Chen. "Let us reason together."

Gravity behaved oddly in an extension cage. Going backward in time, the pull was inward, toward Svetz's navel. Its intensity fluctuated to no known laws.

"I must be getting used to this," Svetz thought.

He found that ominous. Svetz hated time travel. If he was getting used to the odd motion, he had probably given up hope of changing careers.

At least he didn't get sick any more.

"How *did* he talk me into this?"

The extension cage slowed. Gravity dwindled, was gone, came back pointing down.

The inertial calendar read —704. 704 Ante Atomic, seven hundred years before the first nuclear explosion. Through the transparent hull of the extension cage Svetz could see a thousand shades of dark green, green in all directions: a place of obscenely proliferating life. It was the South American jungle where he had found the armadillo.

Svetz donned a filter sac and waited for it to inflate around his head. Then he cut the air system and opened the vents to flood the extension cage with outside air. The ghost had first appeared around 20 PA. If there was a ghost, and if it came, it would probably suffocate in industrial age air.

Svetz took a sonic stun gun from its place on the wall. Subsonics were less material than anaesthetic crystals, more likely to affect a ghost, he told himself.

He pulled the Go-Home lever.

And that was that. Svetz had no controls, only signals. The controls were in the future, with the bulk of the time machine in the Institute building. Now the technicians began bringing him home. They had readings from his last mission. They could make his cage behave as it had then.

Svetz had nothing to do but wait.

Time travel still cost over a million commercials a shot. If the cage simply brought him home now, he was going to feel like an idiot. But then, so would Ra Chen.

He was passing 17 Post Atomic when the haze began to form. Svetz stayed on his back, but he raised the handgun.

It was clearer now, more solid. A dark, voluminous cloak and hood showed behind the pale, translucent outline of a human skeleton. Details were blurred, mercifully perhaps, because the thing was moving too fast, screaming and pleading and gesticulating, all without a sound. It was frantic. It begged Svetz to stop the machine.

Svetz fired the stun weapon.

He kept the stud down until his own head buzzed from the echoes. The apparition screamed what must have been a string of curses, and thereafter ignored him. It wrapped the bones of its hands around the Emergency Stop, braced the bones of its feet against the control panel, and pulled.

The lever didn't move. It was as if fog clung to the control panel.

+46, +47, +48 . . .

Svetz began to relax. The thing was harmless.

He was willing to believe that it was man-shaped, though he could see no trace of the ghostly flesh that must surround the smoky bones. Perhaps he was watching some kind of probability phenomenon. As if the ghost-figure marked where a man might be if there were another man aboard Svetz's extension cage, and its transparency was a measure of just how improbable that was . . . Svetz's head began to ache. Certainly he could not be expected to capture a probability-phenomenon.

The ghost slowly faded, then became clear. It shifted its grip. The white of bones gleamed faintly through dark cloak.

+132, +133, +134 . . .

The ghost came solid in an instant. It pulled the Emergency Stop down hard, turned and leapt.

It was still a skeleton.

Svetz screamed high and shrill, turned and tried to burrow into the hull. He felt the thing land on his back, light and dry and hard. He wailed again. He was in fetal position now, hugging his knees. Bony fingers tugged at his hand, and he screamed and let go of the stun gun. The fingers took it away.

For a long time nothing happened. Svetz waited for the end. Instead he heard slow footsteps, clickings . . .

And a hollow, grating voice that said, "All right, that's enough of that. Roll over."

Small bones prodded Svetz's ribs. He rolled over and opened his eyes.

It was as bad as he'd thought. Worse. The ghost-figure had turned solid, but it was still no more than a mobile skeleton. It stood now with its cloak flung back and a sonic stun gun in its finger bones. Its face was a skull. Far back in the black eye sockets, eyes watched him steadily.

"Stop staring," said the apparition.

It spoke Speech. It spoke Svetz's language. But the

consonants came out mushy, because the thing's skull was lipless.

It chuckled hollowly. "You can see me, can't you? It means you're going to die. When people can see me, it's because they're going to die."

"No," Svetz whispered. His legs were trying to push him back through the wall of the extension cage.

"Stop staring! It's not my fault I'm this way. It was the radiation." The apparition shifted uncomfortably. "What's your name?"

"S-svetz."

"Allow me to introduce myself. I am Doctor Nathaniel Reynolds, the world's first time traveler, and I've decided to hijack your time machine."

Svetz licked his lips. "I don't think so. The first time traveler—"

"I beat him to it. On another line of history, of course. A dead line. My own fault. Have you ever heard of the Cuban missile crisis? The date was nineteen fifty-eight AD, Seventeen Post Atomic, your dating."

"No."

"You're sure? We called it the Short War."

Svetz shook his head.

"Doctor Reynolds" settled himself against the curved wall. He held Svetz's gun steadily on Svetz.

He was not as much a skeleton as Svetz had thought. There was skin over the bones, though the skin itself was the white of bleached bone. In Reynolds's neck there were trachea and gullet as well as the lumpy row of vertebrae.

The rib cage was something else again. Reynolds's ribs were naked bone. Behind the ribs was a narrow torso of flabby white flesh that pulsed like lungs. Torso and abdomen depended from the spine; but daylight showed between the exoskeletal ribs.

The nose and ears were mere holes.

The pelvic bones were sharp as ax blades.

Doctor Reynolds was both hairless and sexless.

He said, "I don't talk well. The only people who can see me and hear me are always about to die. Sometimes they're too sick to concentrate. Sometimes too busy. Sometimes too scared."

"Am I dying?"

Reynolds chuckled. "We'll decide that between us."

"What are you?"

"I'm a ghost. My own fault. But don't laugh. It could happen to you."

Svetz was not thinking of laughing.

"Let me tell you. I was born about a century after the Short War," said Doctor Reynolds. "By then it was obvious the human race was dying. Too many countries had dropped too many bombs in the Short War. Some were cobalt bombs. There was still too much radiation around. Too many mutations, mostly sick and mostly sterile, not to mention disgusting. I was one of the lucky ones."

Svetz said nothing.

"I'd have knocked your teeth out," said the hollow voice. "I really was one of the lucky ones. No brain damage. No gonads, but so what? With all the radiation around I wouldn't have bred true anyway. No organic damage that couldn't be fixed by available medicines. I had to take the pills every day, of course. Would you believe that I once had a pot belly?"

Svetz shook his head.

"A very small pot belly. I had to get rid of it. It hurt. My abdominal muscles couldn't carry the weight. Funny: I've never picked up fat anywhere else. Just the belly, and bones showing through the rest of me."

"How did you get to be a ghost?"

Reynolds laughed, a weak, hollow sound. "Deliberately, and by dint of great effort. There were thousands of us working on it. There wasn't any question that we were doomed. Our best brains, such as we were, were working on time travel. We called it Project Retake. You know what a retake is?"

"Doing a scene over for a sensory."

"That's what we were after. We weren't sure the past could be changed even if we did have time travel. But we had to try it. We did it, too. The time machine was just big enough for me and the scrambler system. They picked me because I only weigh about fifty pounds."

"What did you do?"

"Scrambled the guidance mechanisms of every guided missile in the Union of Soviet Socialist Republics, a week before the Cuban missile crisis. They had to back down and move the missiles out of Cuba. By the time they got their missiles fixed the crisis was over, and they still didn't know what had happened. It must have made them cautious for awhile afterward.

"I monitored it all by radio. I made sure nobody saw me, of course. My appearance is a bit—"

"Right."

"So. Afterward I tried to go home. Not to my own present, but to the new one, the one I'd created. My time machine didn't work. We saved a lot of weight by leaving the power source fixed in the future. Now it was gone.

"I left the machine and went to give myself up. And found out I was gone too . . .

"Well, that's all over now," said Reynolds. He hefted the stunner. The bones of his hands were crossed by narrow strands of muscle. His fingernails were long and ragged. "We're going to put it back the way it was."

"Uh?"

"Using your time machine. Mine wouldn't do it, but yours will. We're going back to seventeen Post Atomic."

"We can't."

"I'll kill you if we don't."

Sventz believed him. When Nathaniel Reynolds gave himself a name, Svetz had stopped seeing him as a supernatural horror. But he was convinced that the bony physicist was mad.

He said, "You don't understand. This isn't a time machine, it's only the extension cage, the part that does the moving. The technicians have to haul me back to the present before they can send me back again."

"You're lying."

"No! Reynolds, there aren't any controls here—just on-off pulses to tell the technicians which way to move me. They can only move me forward now."

"I almost believe you," Reynolds mused. "But I'll still kill you unless one of us thinks of something."

"You're crazy! You'd have to be crazy to want your bombed-out world back!"

The skeleton clacked his teeth. Svetz saw the red of his mouth, horribly incongruous in the white skull. "Svetz, you haven't asked me how long I've been a ghost."

"How long, then?"

"There's no way to measure. Svetz, I'm anchored to seventeen Post Atomic. I wait, I get eight months or so beyond the Cuban missile crisis, and then everything slows down and stops. I think it's been thousands of years. More.

"Can you imagine anything more horrible? It's a frozen world. People like statues. Pigeons nailed to the air. I'm frozen too. I don't get old, I don't get hungry. Sunlight goes right through me. See how white my skin is? And I can't die. I'm not real enough to die. I'd have gone crazy long ago if it weren't for the time machines."

Reynolds's eyes burned black within the pits of his skull. "The time machines. I see them going and coming, Svetz. Some from your line of history, some from others. Yours is the real future, the future I made. But I can ride the others too.

"Mostly I ride them into the past as far as they'll go. That way time passes normally for me, until seventeen Post Atomic rolls around again. I've been through the Middle Ages a dozen times.

"Funny thing, Svetz. I'm invisible to most people. But anyone can see me if he's about to die. Maybe because he's about to leave time entirely; it doesn't matter what line of history he's on, or I'm on." Reynolds laughed. "I think some of them die *because* they see me. Heart failure."

Svetz shuddered. Reynolds was probably right.

Reynolds said, "Not funny, eh? I've been in the future too. Dozens of futures. Svetz, did you know that your time machines go sidewise in time?"

"We had one that did. It was damaged."

"They all do. They wobble. The self-powered ones get lost. The ones that are anchored to their own lines of history, like yours, they always get pulled back, no matter how far they slip across alternate probabilities.

"I've seen some strange futures, Svetz. Paradises. Alien invasions. One where elephants were civilized. I've been in *your* future," Reynolds said bitterly. "Long enough to learn Speech. Long enough to see what you've done to the world I made you."

"What do you mean?"

"What do I mean? Everything's dirty, everything's dead! You killed off everything but yourselves and that grey sludge you eat——"

"Dole yeast."

"Dole yeast. I know a short word that would fit it better. I've watched you ejecting that sludge from your mouths——"

"*What?*"

"I was going backward in time, of course, waiting to slide back to seventeen Post Atomic. The fun goes out of that awfully fast. I don't like hopping time machines into the future, not unless I can get a ride back.

"But I do it anyway. There's always the chance a time machine will wobble across my own line of history. Then I could get off, or even stop the machine. And it paid off, didn't it?"

"I don't understand."

"You haven't looked outside at all, have you, Svetz?"

For the first time, Svetz looked *past* Reynolds . . .

The extension cage rested on a plain of cracked black glass. Nothing grew. Far in the distance was a line of . . . Svetz abruptly realized that it was a rim wall. They were in something like a lunar crater.

"This is your world?"

"That's right. I'm home."

"I can't say I like it much."

Reynolds laughed his hollow, grating laugh. "It's cleaner than your world, Svetz. If I'd known you'd kill off everything on Earth, poison the land and the water and the air . . . well, never mind. We'll fix that."

"What do you mean? All you've got to do is step outside! You're home!"

"But it isn't real. I need you to make it real. This is the only time I've ever been able to affect a time machine. You're my only chance, Svetz."

"But I told you—"

"Svetz. This is a stun gun. It can't hurt anyone, but it can hold you still while I immobilize you. After that, well, I've spent considerable time in medieval torture chambers."

"Wait. Wait. What year did you leave from? What was the date when you left to stop the Short War?"

"Ah, twenty ninety-two. You wouldn't think to look at me that I was only twenty-two years old, would you? I haven't aged since—"

"What date Post Atomic?"

"Let's see. One forty-seven."

The inertial calendar read +134.

"All right. You can hitch a ride on your own time machine! It leaves thirteen years from now. We can't move back in time, but we can jump forward." Svetz reached for the Go-Home. In the same instant his arm became dead meat dropping limply back to his side.

Reynolds said, "But if we tried to go into the future, we'd likely slip sidewise, wouldn't we? And then the pat-

tern of events would have been different, and I wouldn't
exist any more, would I?"

So it was certainly worth a try, thought Svetz. He said,
"What are you going to do, wait thirteen years?"

"If I have to." Reynolds clacked his teeth. Apparently
it was his only expression; it must make do for a smile, a
scowl, a thoughtful look . . . "Hah! I can do better than
that. Svetz, can you get me to Australia? Will this thing
travel in space coordinates?"

"Yes."

"I'm going to change guns." Reynolds stood, examined
the equipment lining the curved wall, selected a weapon.
"A heavy needle gun. It wouldn't kill an elephant, maybe,
but there's anaesthetic enough in here to kill a man."

"Yah," said Svetz. He felt very afraid.

"And now we'll go."

Australia. The eastern coast was a cityscape of streets
and oblong buildings. "It's the only place on Earth that's
even marginally habitable," said Reynolds. "It's mostly
empty now." And he directed Svetz south along the
coast.

He had not stopped talking during the entire flight. He
sprawled motionless as a laboratory exhibit, the gun
propped casually on one kneecap, while he poured out a
steady monologue of reminiscence.

"Of course I have a poor opinion of mankind," he was
saying in answer to one of his own questions. "Why not?
If you'd seen people under stress as often as I have, in
overcrowded hospitals, in torture chambers, on scaffolds
and headsman's blocks, on battlefields—you'd know. People take stress badly. Especially on battlefields.

"Now, I may have a biased viewpoint. I suppose I
should spend more time at square dances and New Year's
Eve parties and palace balls, places where people laugh a

lot, but, Svetz, who would I *talk* to? Nobody can see me or hear me unless he's about to die.

"And then they won't listen. Men bear suffering so badly! And they're so afraid to die. I've tried to tell them how lucky they are, to be able to buy eternal peace at the price of a few hours of agony. I've talked to millions of men and women and children, over tens of thousands of years. The only ones who listen are the children, sometimes. Svetz, are you afraid of death?"

"Yes."

"Idiot."

"Are you sure you know where we're going?"

"Oh, we'll find it, Svetz, don't worry. We're looking for the school."

"A school? What for?"

"You'll see. There's only one school, Svetz. It's far too big for the number of children . . . You know, sometimes the people I talk to seem to recognize me. But then they always behave like idiots. 'Don't take me!' As if I had something to do with it. I've had men offer me gold—how would I carry it? And what the women offer me makes even less sense, if they'd only use their own senses." Reynolds pointed. "There, that wide parkland."

Wide? It was vast, all green grass and the green heads of trees. Svetz was reminded of the jungle where he'd found the armadillo. But this greenery was neater, and there were white buildings showing here and there.

"That's the zoo, that low building. All the real animals are dead, but we have mechanical mockups. There, the athletic field; see the white lines on the grass? Veer right. We want the lower grade schoolyard."

There were children in the schoolyard, but not many, and they weren't playing much. Many were distorted, their deformities obvious even at this altitude. One nine year old was terribly thin; he looked like a small ambulatory skeleton.

"Hold her steady," said Reynolds. "Open the door."

"No!" Suddenly Svetz understood.

"Open the door." The bore of Reynolds's gun looked straight into Svetz's eyes. Svetz opened the door.

When Reynolds turned to the door, Svetz jumped him.

His dead arm threw him off balance. Reynolds's gun butt caught him under the jaw. Svetz fell back with lights exploding in his head.

When his head cleared, Reynolds was braced in the doorway. Svetz struggled to his knees.

Reynolds fired into the playground.

Svetz staggered toward him with his good hand outstretched.

Reynolds fired again. Then he noticed Svetz and brought the gun around.

Svetz lurched forward to catch the muzzle.

Reynolds fought madly to turn the gun. He couldn't. Svetz, weak as a kitten and ready to die, was still too strong for him. When Reynolds suddenly kicked Svetz under the jaw, it was like being hit with foam plastic.

Six feet tall and a fifty pound weakling. Svetz jerked the gun toward him, out of Reynolds's grip, and threw it behind him. Reynolds staggered helplessly after it. Svetz reached out and took him by the neck.

If he closed his fist, Reynolds would be dead. There was no muscle to protect his windpipe.

Svetz looked down.

The skeleton boy was sprawled beside a green bench, surrounded by boys and girls and small indeterminate beings. He looked dead. Svetz wasted some time trying to think of something to do. Then he moved two levers with his foot.

Gravity changed. Reynolds struggled furiously for a moment; and then Svetz's hand was empty. Something foggy seemed to be tugging at the Emergency Stop. Svetz watched it fade.

"But then he got away with it," said Ra Chen.

Svetz shrugged. "I did my best to stop him."

"You don't get it. He killed *himself*. He stopped himself from ever going back in time to stop the Short War."

Svetz nodded.

"Then—we aren't real! The Short War happened, and Reynolds's line of history happened, and ours didn't! So how can you be here at all?"

"The time machine pulled me home. An extension cage can't get lost, not if it's anchored to its own present."

Ra Chen's eyes were haunted. "But if Reynolds aborted our past, if we don't have a history any more, then—"

"Metaphysics! What if we *aren't* real! What if we never *were* real! Sir, you feel real, don't you? So do I. We can always tell ourselves that Project Retake went ahead without Reynolds."

"But—"

"Or maybe the boy lived. He had no hair and practically no scalp. If Reynolds shot him in the head, the anaesthetic crystal would just ricochet off his skull, right? And knock him out."

"Um. I like that. If the kid was dead at age nine, Reynolds would have disappeared, right? Wrong, futz it!" Ra Chen snarled. "If he made himself unreal, he made you unreal too. Why shouldn't you go on seeing him?"

"Come here a minute." Svetz pulled at Ra Chen's arm, without effect; but after a moment Ra Chen followed him voluntarily.

Beyond the glass wall that fronted the ITR building, half a dozen broken buildings surrounded the broken corpse of a bird. The bird was several blocks long and several weeks dead.

"Now, don't you have enough to worry about besides whether you're real or not?"

"Futz, yes. We've got to do something about that roc," said Ra Chen. "There it lies, in full view of the United Nations Palace . . ."

FLASH CROWD

I

From edge to edge and for all of its length, from Central Los Angeles through Beverly Hills and West Los Angeles and Santa Monica to the sea, Wilshire Boulevard was a walkway.

Once there had been white lines on concrete, and raised curbs to stop the people from interfering with the cars. Now the lines were gone, and much of the concrete was covered with soil and grass. There were even a few trees. Concrete strips had been left for bicycles, and wider places for helicopters carrying cargo too big for the displacement booths.

Wilshire was wide for a walkway. People seemed to hug the edges, even those on bikes and motor skates. A boulevard built for cars was too big for mere people.

Outlines of the street still showed through. Ridges in the grass marked where curbs had been, with breaks where there had been driveways. Some stretches in Westwood had a concrete center divider. The freeway ramps were unchanged and unused. Someday the city would do something about them.

Jerryberry Jensen lived in what had been a seaside motel halfway between Bakersfield and San Francisco. On long-ago summer nights the Shady Rest had been packed with transients at ten dollars a head. Now it made a dandy apartment house, with swimming pool and everything, including a displacement booth outside the manager's office.

There was a girl in the booth when Jerryberry left his apartment. He glimpsed long, wavy brown hair and the shape of her back in the instant before she disappeared. Janice Wolfe. Too bad she hadn't waited . . . but she hadn't even seen him.

Nobody was ever around the booths long enough to say hello to. You could meet someone by hovering outside the booths, but what would they think?

Meeting people was for the clubs.

A displacement booth was a glass cylinder with a rounded top. The machinery that made the magic was invisible, buried beneath the booth. Coin slots and a telephone dial were set into the glass at sternum level.

Jerryberry inserted his CBA credit card below the coin slots. He dialled by punching numbered buttons. Withdrawing the credit card closed a circuit. An eyeblink later he was in an office in the Central Broadcasting Association building in Downtown Los Angeles.

The office was big and empty. Only once in an aeon was all that empty space ever used; though several score of newstapers saw it for a few seconds each day. One wall was lined with displacement booths. A curved desk down at the end was occupied by Jerryberry's boss.

George Bailey was fat from too much sitting, and darkly tanned by the Nevada sun. He commuted to work every morning via the long distance booths at Los Angeles International. Today he waved at Jerryberry without speaking. Routine, then. Jerryberry chose one of several cameras and slung the padded strap over his shoulder. He studied several lists of numbers posted over the table before picking one.

He turned and moved to avoid three more newstapers stepping out of booths. They nodded, he nodded, they passed. As he reached for a booth door, a woman flicked in in front of him. Rush hour. He smiled at her and stepped over to the next booth, consulted the list, dialed and was gone.

He had not spoken to anyone that morning.

The east end of Wilshire Boulevard was a most ordinary T-intersection between high, blocky buildings. Jerryberry looked around even as he was dialing. Nothing newsworthy? No. He was two blocks away, and dialing.

He punched the numbered buttons with a ball point pen, when he remembered. Nonetheless his index finger was calloused.

The streets of the inner city were empty, this early. In a minute or so Jerryberry was in sight of the freeway. He stepped out of the booth to watch trucks and bulldozers covering this part of the Pasadena-Harbor Freeway with topsoil. Old Machines Find New Use—but others were covering the event. He moved on.

The booths were all identical. He might have been in a full-vision theater, watching scenes flick around him. He was used to the way things jerked about. He flicked west on Wilshire, waiting for something to happen.

It was a cheap, effective way to gather news. At a chocolate dollar per jump per man, CBA could afford to support a score of wandering newstapers in addition to the regular staff. They earned low salaries, plus a bonus for each news item, plus a higher bonus per item used. The turnover was high. It had been higher before CBA learned not to jumble the numbers at random. An orderly progression down a single street was easier on the mind and nerves.

Jerryberry Jansen knew every foot of Wilshire. At twenty-eight he was old enough to remember cars and trucks and traffic lights. When the city changed, it was the streets that had changed most.

He watched Wilshire change as he dialed.

At the old hat-shaped Brown Derby they were converting the parking lot into a miniature golf course. About time they did something with all that wasted space. He queried Bailey, but Bailey wasn't interested.

The Miracle Mile was a landscaped section. Suddenly there were people: throngs of shoppers, so thick that many preferred to walk a block instead of waiting for a booth. They seemed stratified, with the older people hugging the curbs and the teens taking the middle of the street. Jerryberry had noticed it before. As a child he'd been trained to cross only in the crosswalks, with the light. Sometimes his training came back, and he found himself looking both ways before he could step out from the curb.

He moved on, west, following the list of numbers that was his beat.

The Mall had been a walkway when displacement booths were no more than a theorem in quantum mechanics. Dips in the walk showed where streets had crossed; but the Santa Monica Mall had always been a sanctuary for pedestrians and window shoppers. Here were several blocks of shops and restaurants and theaters, low buildings that did not block the sky.

Displacement booths were thick here. People swarmed constantly around and in and out of them. Some travelers carried fold-up bicycles. Many wore change purses. From noon onward there was always the tension of too many people trying to use the same space for the same purpose.

The argument started outside Penney's Department Store. At the time, one could only see that the police officer was being firm and the woman—middle-aged, big and brawny—was screaming at the top of her lungs. A crowd grew, not because anyone gave a damn but because the two were blocking the walkway. People had to stream around them.

Some of them stopped to see what was happening.

Many later remembered hearing the policeman repeating, "Madam, I place you under arrest on suspicion of shoplifting. Anything you say—" in a voice that simply did not carry. If the officer had used his shock stick then, nothing more would have happened. Maybe. Then again, he might have been mobbed. Already the crowd blocked the entire Mall, and too many of them were shouting—genial or sarcastic suggestions, random insults, and a thousand variations of "Get out of my way!" and "I can't, you idiot!" —for any to be heard at all.

At 12:55 Jerryberry Jansen flicked in, looked quickly about him while his hands were re-inserting his credit card. His eyes registered the ancient shops at the end of the Mall, lingered a moment on the entrance to Romanoff's. Anyone newsworthy? Sometimes they came, the Big Names, for the cuisine or the publicity. No?—passed on, jumped to the crowd in front of Penney's, two blocks down.

There were booths nearer, but he didn't know the numbers offhand. Jerryberry picked up his card and stepped out of the booth. He signalled the studio but didn't bother to report. Circumstantial details he could give later. But he turned on his camera, and the event was now . . . real.

He jogged the two blocks. Whatever was happening might end without him.

A young, bemused face turned at Jerryberry's hail. "Excuse me, sir. Can you tell me how this started?"

"Nope. Sorry. I just got here," said the young man; and he strolled off. He would be edited from the tape. But other heads were turning, noticing the arrival of—

A lean young man with an open, curious, friendly face, topped by red-blond hair curly as cotton. A tiny mike at his lips, a small plug in one ear, a coin purse at his belt. In his hands, a heavy gyrostabilized TV camera equipped with a directional mike.

A newstaper. One pair of eyes turned for an instant too

long. The woman swung her purse. The policeman's arm came up too late to block the purse, which bounced solidly off his head. Something heavy in that purse.

The policeman dropped.

Things happened very fast.

Jerryberry talked rapidly to himself while he panned the camera. Occasional questions in his earpiece did not interrupt the flow of his report, though they guided it. The gyrostabilized camera felt like a live thing in his hands. It followed the woman with the heavy purse as she pushed her way through the crowd, shot Jerryberry a venomous look, and ran for a displacement booth. It watched someone break a jeweler's window, snatch up a handful of random jewelry and run. The directional mike picked up the scream of an alarm.

The police officer was still down.

Jerryberry went to help him. It occurred to him that of those present, the policeman was most likely to know what had been going on. The voice in his earpiece told him that others were on their way, even as his eye found them leaving the booths: faces he knew on men carrying cameras like his own. He knelt beside the policeman.

"Officer, can you tell me what happened?"

The uniformed man looked up with hurt, bewildered eyes. He said something that the directional mike picked up, but Jerryberry's ears lost it in the crowd noise. He heard it later on the news. "Where's my hat?"

Jerryberry repeated, "What happened here?"

—While a dozen CBA men around him were interviewing the crowd, and police were pouring out of the displacement booths. The flow of blue uniforms looked like far more than they were. They had to use their shock sticks to get through the crowd.

Some of the spectator/shopper/strollers had decided to leave. A wise decision, but impractical. The nearest booths could not be used at all. They held passengers cased in glass, each trying to get his door open against the press of the mob. Every few seconds one would give up and flick out, and another trapped passenger would be pushing at the door.

For blocks around, there was no way to get into a displacement booth. As fast as anyone left a booth, someone else would flick in. Most were nondescript citizens who came to gape. A few carried big cardboard rectangles carelessly printed in flourescent colors, often with the paint still wet. A different few, nondescript otherwise, had rocks in their pockets.

For Jerryberry, kneeling above the felled policeman and trying to get audible sense out of him, it all seemed to explode. He looked up and it was a riot.

"It's a riot," he said, awed. The directional mike picked it up.

The crowd surged, and he was moving. He looked back, trying to see if the policeman had gained his feet. If he hadn't, he could be hurt . . . but the crowd surged away. In this mob there was no conservation of matter; there were sources and sinks in it, and today all the sinks were sources. The flow had to go somewhere.

A young woman pushed herself close to Jerryberry. Her eyes were wide, her hair was wild. A kind of rage, a kind of joy made her face a battlefield. "Legalize direct current stimulus!" she screamed at him. She lunged and caught the snout of Jerryberry's camera and mike, pulled it around to face her. *"Legalize wireheading!"*

Jerryberry wrenched the camera free. He turned it toward the big display window in Penney's. The glass was gone. Men crawled in the display window, looting. Jerryberry held the camera high, taking pictures of them over the bobbing heads. He had the scene for a moment—and then three signs shot up in front of the camera. One said TANSTAAFL, and one bore a mushroom cloud and the words POWER CORRUPTS! and Jerryberry never read the third because the crowd surged again and he had to scramble to keep his feet. There were men and women and children being trampled here. He could be one of them.

How had it happened? He'd seen it all, but he didn't understand.

He tried to keep the camera over his head. He got a big, brawny, hairy type carrying a stack of TVs under his arm, half a dozen twenty-inch sets almost an inch thick. The thief saw the camera facing him, and the solemn face beneath, and he roared and lunged toward Jerryberry.

Jerryberry abruptly realized that there were people here who would not want to be photographed. The big man had dropped his TVs and was plowing toward him with murder on his face. Jerryberry had to drop his camera to get away. When he looked back, the big man was smashing the camera against a lamp post.

Idiot. The scene was on tape now, in the CBA buildings in Los Angeles and in Denver.

The riot splashed outward. Jerryberry perforce went with it. He concentrated on keeping his feet.

II

The explosive growth of the Mall Riot has taken law enforcement agencies by surprise. Police have managed to hold the perimeter and are letting people through the lines, but necessarily in small numbers . . .

The screen showed people being filtered through a police blockade, one at a time. They looked tired, stunned. One had two pockets full of stolen wristwatches. He did not protest when they confiscated the watches and led him away. A blank-eyed girl maintained a death grip on a rough wooden stick glued to a cardboard rectangle. The cardboard was crumpled and torn, the Day-Glo colors smeared.

Meanwhile all displacement booths in the area have been shut down from outside. The enclosed area includes fourteen city blocks. Viewers are warned away from the following areas . . . These scenes were taken by CBA helicopter . . .

Most of the street lights were out. Those left cast monstrous shadows through the Mall. Orange flames flickered in the windows of a furniture store. Dimunitive figures, angered by spotlights in the helicopter, pointed and shouted silently into the camera viewpoint. The deep, earnest voice went on: *We are getting no transmissions from inside the affected area. A dozen CBA newsmen and an undisclosed number of police in the area have not been heard from . . .*

Many of the rioters are armed. A CBA helicopter was shot down early today, but was able to crashland beyond the perimeter. Close shot of a helicopter smashed against a brick wall. Two men being carried out on stretchers, in obvious haste. *The source of weapons is not known. Police conjecture that they may have been looted from Kerr's Sport Shop, which has a branch in the Mall . . .*

How did it all start?

The square brown face looking out of the tridee screen was known throughout the English-speaking world. When news was good that wide mouth would smile enormously, the filter cigarette in the middle of it smoldering delicately between white front teeth. It was not smiling now. That expression was more than earnest; it was shaken.

Jerryberry Jansen looked back with no expression at all.

He had thrown away his camera and seen it destroyed. He had dropped his coin purse and ear mike into a trash can. Not being a newsman was a good idea during the Mall Riot. Now, an hour after the police had let him through, he was still wandering aimlessly. He had no goal. Almost, he had thrown away his identity.

He stood in front of an appliance store window, watching TV. The deep, precise voice of Wash Evans was audible through the glass—barely.

How did it all start?

Evans vanished, and Jerryberry watched scenes taken by his own camera. A milling crowd, mostly trying to get past a disturbance . . . a blue uniformed man, a brawny woman with a heavy purse . . . *The officer was trying to arrest a suspected shoplifter, who has not been identified, when this man appeared on the scene . . .*

Picture of Jerryberry Jansen, camera held high, caught in the view of another CBA camera.

Barry Jerome Jansen, a roving newstaper. It was he who reported the disturbance— The woman swung her purse. The policeman went down, his arms half-raised as if to hide his head. *—and reported it as a riot, to this man—* Bailey, at his desk in the CBA building. Jerryberry twitched. Sooner or later he would have to report to Bailey. And explain where his camera had gone.

He'd picked up some good footage, and it was being used. A string of bonuses waiting for him . . . unless Bailey docked him for the cost of the camera . . .

George Lincoln Bailey sent in a crew to cover the disturbance. He also put the report on teevee, practically live, editing it as it came. At this point anyone with a TV, anywhere in the United States, could see the violence being filmed by a dozen veteran CBA newstapers.

The square dark face returned. *And then it all blew up. The population of the Mall expanded catastrophically, and they all started breaking things. Why?* Wash Evans flashed a white grin with a cigarette in it. *Well, it seems that there are people who like riots.*

Jerryberry cocked his head. He had never heard it put quite like that.

Now that seems silly. Who would want to be caught in a riot? Wash Evans had long, expressive fingers with pink nails. He began ticking off items on his fingers. *First, more police, to stop what's being reported as a riot. Second, more newstapers. Third, anyone who wants publicity—* On the screen behind Wash Evans, signs shot out of a sea of moving heads. A girl's face swelled enormously, so close she seemed all mouth, and shrieked, "Legalize wireheading!"

Anyone with a cause. Anyone who wants the ear of the public. There are newsmen here, man! And cameras! And publicity!

Behind Evans the scene jumped. That was Angela Monk coming out of a displacement booth! Angela Monk the semiporno movie actress, very beautiful in a dress of loose-mesh net made from white braided yarn, very self-possessed in the split second before she saw what she'd flicked into. She tried to dodge back inside, and to hell with the free coverage. A yell went up; hands pulled the door open before she could dial again; other hands pulled her out.

Then there are people who have never seen a riot in person. A lot of them came. What they think about it now is something else again.

Now, all of these might not be a big fat percentage of the public. How many people would be dumb enough to come watch a riot? But that little percentage, they all came at once, from all over the United States and some other places too. And the more there were, the bigger the crowd got, the louder it got—the better it looked to the looters. Evans folded down his remaining finger. *And the looters came from everywhere too. These days you can get from anywhere to anywhere in three flicks.*

Scenes shifted in Evans's background. Store windows being smashed, to a subdued wail of sirens. A CBA helicopter thrashing about in midair. An ape of a man carrying stolen tridees under one arm. Evans looked soberly out at his audience. *So there you have it. An unidentified shoplifting suspect, a roving newsman who reported a minor disturbance as a riot—*

"Good God!" Jerryberry Jansen was jolted completely awake. "They're blaming me!"

"They're blaming me too," said George Bailey. He ran his hands through his hair, glossy shoulder length white hair that grew in a fringe around a dome of suntanned scalp. "You're second in the chain. I'm third. If only they could find the woman who hit the cop!"

"They haven't?"

"Not a sign of her. Jansen, you look like hell."

"I should have changed suits. This one's been through a riot." Jerryberry's laugh sounded forced, and was. "I'm glad you waited. It must be way past your quitting time."

"Oh, no. We've been in conference all night. We only broke up about twenty minutes ago. Damn Wash Evans anyway! Have you heard—"

"I heard some of it."

"A couple of the Directors want to fire him. Not unlike the ancient technique of using gasoline to put out a fire. There were some even wilder suggestions. —Have you seen a doctor?"

"I'm not hurt. Just bruised . . . and tired, and hungry, come to think of it. I lost my camera."

"You're lucky you got out alive."

"I know."

George Bailey seemed to brace himself. "I hate to be the one to tell you. We're going to have to let you go, Jansen."

"What? You mean fire me?"

"Yah. Public pressure. I won't make it pretty for you. Wash Evans's instant documentary has sort of torn things open. It seems you caused the Mall Riot. It would be nice if we could say we fired you for it."

"But, but I *didn't!*"

"Yes you did. Think about it." Bailey wasn't looking at him. "So did I. CBA may have to fire me too."

"Now—" Jerryberry stopped, started over. "Now wait a minute. If you're saying what I think you're saying— But what about freedom of the press?"

"We talked about that too."

"I didn't exaggerate what was happening. I reported a, a *disturbance*. When it turned into a riot I called it a riot. Did I lie about anything? *Anything?*"

"Oh, in a way," Bailey said in a tired voice. "You've got your choice about where to point that camera. You pointed it where there was fighting, didn't you? And I picked out the most exciting scenes. When we both finished it looked like a small riot. Fighting everywhere! Then everyone who wanted to be in the middle of a small riot came flicking in, just like Evans said, and in thirty seconds we had a large riot.

"You know what somebody suggested? A time limit on news. A law against reporting anything until twenty-four hours after it happens. Can you imagine anything sillier? For ten thousand years people have been working to send news further and faster, and now— Oh, hell, Jansen, *I* don't know about freedom of the press. But the riot's still going on, and everyone's blaming you. You're fired."

"Thanks." Jerryberry surged out of his chair on what felt like the last of his strength. Bailey moved just as fast, but by the time he got around the desk Jerryberry was inside a booth, dialing.

He stepped out into a warm black night. He felt sick and miserable and very tired. It was two in the morning. His paper suit was torn and crumpled and clammy.

George Bailey stepped out of the booth behind him. "Thought so. Now, Jansen, let's talk sense."

"How did you know I'd be here?"

"I had to guess you'd come straight home. Jansen, you won't suffer for this. You may make money on it. CBA wants an exclusive interview on the riot, your viewpoint. Thirty-five hundred bucks."

"Screw that."

"In addition, there's two weeks severance pay and a stack of bonusses. We used a lot of your tape. And when this blows over, I'm sure we'll want you back."

"Blows over, huh?"

"Oh, it will. News gets stale awfully fast these days. I know. Jansen, why don't you want thirty-five hundred bucks?"

"You'd play me up as the man who started the Mall Riot. Make me more valuable. —Wait a minute. Who have you got in mind for the interview?"

"Who else?"

"Wash Evans!"

"He's fair. You'd get your say." Bailey considered him. "Let me know if you change your mind. You'd have a chance to defend yourself, and you'd get paid besides."

"No chance."

"All right." Bailey went.

III

For Eric Jansen and his family, displacement booths came as a disaster.

At first he didn't see it that way. He was twenty-eight (and Barry Jerome Jansen was three) when JumpShift Inc. demonstrated the augmented tunnel diode effect on a lead brick. He watched it on television. He found the prospects exciting.

Eric Jansen had never worked for a salary. He wrote. Poetry and articles and a few short stories, highly polished, admired by a small circle of readers, sold at infrequent intervals to low-paying markets which he regarded as prestigious. His money came from inherited stocks. If he had invested in JumpShift then—but millions could tell that sad story. It was too risky, then.

He was thirty-one when commercial displacement booths began to be sold for cargo transport. He was not caught napping. Many did not believe that the magic could work, until suddenly the phenomenon was changing their world. But Eric Jansen looked into the phenomenon very carefully.

He found that there was an inherent limitation on the augmented tunnel diode effect. Teleportation over a difference in altitude made for drastic temperature changes: a drop of seven degrees Fahrenheit for every mile upward, and vice versa, due to conservation of energy. Conservation of momentum, plus the rotation of the Earth, put a distance limit on lateral travel. A passenger flicking east would find himself kicked upward by the difference between his velocity and the Earth's. Flicking west, he would be slapped down. North and south, he would be kicked sideways.

Cargo and passenger displacement booths were springing up in every city in America. But Eric Jansen knew that they would always be restricted to short distances. Even a ten mile jump would be bumpy. A passenger flicking halfway around the equator would have to land running—at half a mile per second.

JumpShift stock was sky-high. Eric Jansen decided it must be overpriced.

He considered carefully, then made his move.

He sold all of his General Telephone stock. If anyone wanted to talk to someone, he would just *go*, wouldn't he? A displacement booth took no longer than a phone call.

He tried to sell his General Motors, wisely, but everyone else wisely made the same decision, and the price fell like a dead bird. At least he got something back on the stock he owned in motorcycle and motor scooter companies. Later he regretted that. It developed that people rode motorcycles and scooters for fun. Now, with the streets virtually empty, they were buying more than ever.

Still, he had fluid cash now—and the opportunity to make a killing.

Airline stock had dropped with other forms of transportation. Before the general public could realize its mistake, Eric Jansen invested every dime in airlines and aircraft companies. The first displacement booths in any city were links to the airport. That lousy half-hour drive from the center of town, the heavy taxi fare in, were gone forever. And the booths couldn't compete with the airlines themselves!

Of course you still had to check in early—and the planes only took off at specified times—and they still lost your luggage—

What it amounted to was that plane travel was easier, but short-distance travel was infinitely easier. (Infinitely. Try dividing any ten-minute drive by zero.) And planes still crashed. Cassettes had copped the entertainment market, so that television was mostly news these days; you didn't have to *go* anywhere to find out what was happening. Just turn on the TV.

A plane flight wasn't worth the hassle.

As for the telephone stock, people still made long distance calls. They tended to phone first before they went visiting. They would give out a phone number where they would not give out a displacement booth number.

The airlines survived, somehow, but they paid rock-bottom dividends. Barry Jerome Jansen grew up poor in the midst of a boom period. His father hated the displacement booths, and used them, because there was nothing else.

Jerryberry accepted that irrational hatred as part of his father's personality. He did not share it. He hardly noticed the displacement booths. They were part of the background. The displacement booths were the most important part of a newstaper's life; and still he hardly noticed their existence.

Until the day they turned on him.

IV

In the morning there were messages stored in his phone. He heard them out over breakfast.

114

Half a dozen news services and tapezines wanted exclusives on the riot. One call was from Bailey at CBA. The price had gone up to four thousand. The others did not mention price; but one was from *Playboy*.

That gave him furiously to thought. *Playboy* paid high, and they liked unpopular causes.

Three people wanted to murder him. On two of them the TV was blanked. The third was a greying dowdy woman, all fat and hate and disappointed hopes, who showed him a kitchen knife and started to tell him what she wanted to do with it. Jerryberry cut her off, shuddering. He wondered if any of them could possibly get hold of his displacement booth number.

There was a check in the mail. Severance pay and a bonus from CBA. So that was that.

He was setting the dishes in the dishwasher when the phone rang. He hesitated, decided to answer . . .

It was Janice Wolfe—a pretty oval face, brown eyes, a crown of long, wavy, soft brown hair—and not an anonymous killer. She lost her smile as she saw him. "You look grim. Could you use some cheering up?"

"Yes!" Jerryberry said fervently. "Come on over. Apartment six, booth number—"

"I live here, remember?"

He laughed. He'd forgotten. You got used to people living anywhere and everywhere. George Bailey lived in Nevada; he commuted to work every morning in three flicks, using the long distance displacement booths at Las Vegas and Los Angeles International airports.

Those long distance booths had saved the airlines—after his father had dribbled away most of his stocks to feed his family. They had been operating only two years. And, come to think of it—

Doorbell.

Over coffee, he told Janice about the riot. She listened sympathetically, asking occasional questions to draw him out. At first Jerryberry tried to talk entertainingly, until he realized, first that she wasn't indulging in a spectator sport, and second, that she knew all about the riot already.

She knew he'd been fired, too. "That's why I called. They put it on the morning news," she told him.

"It figures."

"What are you going to do now?"

"Get drunk. Alone if I have to. Would you like to spend a lost weekend with me?"

She hesitated. "You'll be bitter."

"Yah, I probably will. Not fit to live with. —Hey, Janice. Do you know anything about how the long distance displacement booths work?"

"No. Should I?"

"The Mall Riot couldn't have happened without the long distance booths. That damn Wash Evans might at least have mentioned the fact . . . . except that I only just thought of it myself. Funny. There hasn't *ever* been a riot that happened that quick."

"I'll come with you," Janice decided.

"What? *Good.*"

"You don't start drinking this early in the morning, do you?"

"I guess not. Are you free today?"

"Every day, during summer. I teach school."

"Oh. So what'll we do? San Diego Zoo?" he suggested at random.

"Sounds like fun."

They made no move to get up. It felt peaceful in Jerryberry's tiny kitchen nook. There was still coffee.

"You could get a bad opinion of me this way. I feel like tearing things up."

"Go ahead."

"I mean it."

"Me too," she said serenely. "You need to tear things up. Fine, go ahead. After that you can try to put your life back together."

116

"Just what kind of school do you teach?"

Janice laughed. "Fifth grade."

There was quiet.

"You know what the punch line is? Wash Evans wants to interview me! After that speech he made!"

"That sounds like a good idea," she said surprisingly. "Gives you a chance to give your side of the story. You didn't *really* cause the Mall Riot, did you?"

"No!. . . no. Janice, he's just too damn good. He'd make mincemeat of me. By the time he got through I'd be The Man Who Caused The Mall Riot, in every English-speaking country in the world, and some others too, because he gets translations—"

"He's just a *commentator*."

Jerryberry started to laugh.

"He makes it look so easy," he said. "A hundred million eyes out there, watching him, and he knows it. Have you ever seen him self-conscious? Have you ever heard him at a loss for words? My dad used to say it about writing, but it's true for Wash Evans. The hardest trick in the world is to make it look easy, so easy that any clod thinks he can do it just as well.

"Hell, *I* know what caused the Mall Riot. The news program, yes. He's right there. But the long distance displacement booth did it too. Control those and we could stop that kind of riot from ever happening again. —But what could I tell Wash Evans about it? What do I know about displacement booths?"

"Well, what *do* you know?"

Jerryberry Jansen looked into his coffee cup for a long time. Presently he said, "I know how to find out things. I know how to find out who knows most about what, and then go ask. Legwork. They *hammered* at it in the journalism classes. I know legwork."

He looked up and met her eyes. Then he lunged across the table to reach the phone.

"Hello? Oh, hi, Jansen. Changed your mind?"

"Yes, but—"

"Good, good! I'll put you through to—"

"*Yes, but!*"

"Oh. Okay, go ahead."

"I want some time to do some research."

"Now, damn it, Jansen, you know that time is just what we don't have! Old news is no news. What kind of research?"

"Displacement booths."

"Why that? Never mind, it's your business. How much time?"

"How much can you afford?"

"Damn little."

"Bailey, CBA upped my price to four thousand this morning. How come?"

"You didn't see it? It's on every screen in the country. The rioters broke through the police line. They've got a good section of Venice now, and there are about twice as many of them, because the police didn't shut down the displacement booths in the area until about twenty minutes too late. Twenty minutes!" Bailey seemed actually to be grinding his teeth. "We held off reporting the breakthrough until they could do it. *We* did. ABS reported it live on all stations. *That's* where all the new rioters came from."

"Then . . . it looks like the Mall Riot is going to last a little longer."

"That it does. And you want more time. Things are working out, aren't they?" Then, "Sorry. Those ABS bastards. How much time do you want?"

"As much as I can get. A week."

"You've *got* to be kidding. You maybe can get twenty-four hours, only I can't make the decision. Why don't you talk to Evans himself?"

"Fine. Put him on."

The TV went on HOLD. Pale blue flow patterns

floated upward in what had become a twenty-inch Kaliro-scope. Waiting, Jerryberry said, "If this riot gets any bigger I could be more famous than Hitler."

Janice set his coffee beside him. She said, "Or Mrs. O'Leary's cow."

The screen came on. "Jansen, can you get over here right now? Wash Evans wants to talk to you in person."

"Okay." Jerryberry clicked off. He felt a thrumming inside him . . . as if he felt the motion of the world, and the world were spinning faster and faster. Surely things were happening fast . . .

Janice said, "No lost weekend."

"Not yet, love. Have you any idea what you've let me in for? I may not sleep for days. I'll have to find out what teleportation is, what it does . . . where do I start?"

"Wash Evans. You'd better get moving."

"Right." He bolted his coffee in three swift gulps. "Thanks. Thanks for coming over, thanks for jarring me off the dime. We'll see how it works out." He went, pulling on a coat.

Wash Evans was five feet four inches tall. People sometimes forgot that size was invisible in a TV closeup. In the middle of a televised interview, when the camera was flashing back and forth between two angry faces, then the deep, sure voice and the dark, mobile, expressive face of Wash Evans could be devastatingly convincing.

Wash Evans looked up at Jerryberry Jansen and said, "I've been wondering if I owe you an apology."

"Take your time," said Jerryberry. He finished buttoning his coat.

"I don't. Fact is, I psyched out the Mall Riot as best I knew how, and I think I did it right. I didn't tell the great unwashed public you caused it all. I just told it like it happened."

119

"You left some things out."

"All right, now we've got something to talk about. Sit down."

They sat. Their faces were level now. Jerryberry said, "This present conversation is not for publication, and is not to be considered an interview. I have an interview to sell. I don't want to undercut myself."

"I accept your terms on behalf of the network. We'll give you a tape of this conversation."

"I'm making my own." Jerryberry tapped his inside pocket, which clicked.

Wash Evans grinned. "Of course you are, my child. Now, what did I miss?"

"Displacement booths."

"Well, *sure*. If the booths had been cut off earlier—"

"If the booths didn't exist."

"You're kidding. No, you're not. Jansen, that's a wishing horse. Displacement booths are here to stay."

"I know. But think about this. Newstapers have been around longer than displacement booths. Roving newstapers, like me—we've been using the booths since they were invented."

"So?"

"Why didn't the Mall Riot happen earlier?"

"I see what you mean. Hmm. The airport booths?"

"Yah."

"Jansen, are you actually going to face the great unwashed TV public and tell them to give up long distance displacement booths?"

"No. I . . . don't know just what I have in mind. That's why I want some time. I want to know more."

"Uh huh," said Evans, and waited.

Jerryberry said, "Turn it around. Are you going to try to talk the public into giving up news programs?"

"No. Maybe to put some restrictions on newstaping practices. We're *too* fast these days. A machine won't

120

work without friction. Neither does a civilization . . . But we'd ruin the networks, wouldn't we?"

"You'd cut your own throat."

"OH, *I'd* be out." Evans mashed out a cigarette. "Take away the news broadcasts, and they wouldn't have anything left to sell but educational TV. Nothing to sell but toys and breakfast cereal. Jansen, I don't know."

"Good," said Jerryberry.

"You question my dispassionate judgment?" Evans chuckled in his throat. "I'm on *both* sides. Suppose we do an interview live, at ten tonight. That'll give you twelve hours—"

"Twelve hours!"

"That's enough, isn't it? You want to research teleportation. I want to get this in while people are still interested in the riot. Not just for the ratings, but because we both have something to say." Jerryberry tried to interrupt, but Evans overrode him. "We'll advance you a thousand, and three more if we do the interview. Nothing if we don't. That'll get you back on time."

Jerryberry accepted it. "One thing. Can you make Bailey forget to cancel my CBA card for awhile? I may have to do a lot of traveling."

"I'll tell him. I don't know if he'll do it."

V

He flicked in at Los Angeles International, off-center in a long curved row of displacement booths: upright glass cylinders with rounded tops, no different from the booths on any street corner. On the opposite wall, a good distance away, large red letters said *TWA.* He stood a moment, thinking. Then he dialed again.

He was home, at the Shady Rest. He dialed again.

He was near the end of the row—and a different row,

with no curve to it. And the opposite wall bore the emblem of United.

Ther terminal was empty except for one man in a blue uniform who was waxing the floor.

Jerryberry stepped out. For upwards of a minute he watched the line of booths. People flicked in at random. Generally they did not even look up. They would dial a long string of digits—sometimes making a mistake, snarling something and starting over—and be gone. There were so many that the booths themselves seemed to be flickering.

He took several seconds of it on the Minox.

Beneath the United emblem was a long, long row of empty counters with scales between them, for luggage. The terminal was spotless—and empty, unused. Haunted by a constant flow of ghosts.

A voice behind him said, "You want something?"

"Is there a manager's office?"

The uniformed man pointed down an enormous length of corridor. "The maintenance section's down that way, where the boarding area used to be. I'll call ahead, let them knew you're coming."

The corridor was long, unnecessarily long, and it echoed. The walk was eating up valuable time . . . and then an open cart came from the other end, silently pulled up alongside him. A straight-backed old man in a one-button business lounger said, "Hello. Want a ride?"

"Thanks." Jerryberry climbed aboard. He handed over his CBA credit card. "I'm doing some research for a, a documentary of sorts. What can you tell me about the long distance booths?"

"Anything you like. I'm Nils Kjerulf. I helped install these booths, and I've been working on them ever since."

"How do they work?"

"Where do I start? Do you know how a normal booth works?"

"Sure. The load isn't supposed to exist at all between

the two endpoints. Like the electron in a tunnel diode."
An answer right out of the science section of any tapezine.
Beyond that he could fake it.

This Nils Kjerulf was lean and ancient, with deep
smile wrinkles around his eyes and mouth. His hair was
thick and white. He said, "They had to give up that
theory. When you're sending a load to Mars, say, you
have to assume that *something* exists in the ten minutes
or so it takes the load to make the trip. Conservation
of energy."

"All right. What is it?"

"For ten minutes it's a kind of super-neutrino. That's
what they tell me. I'm not a physicist. I was in business administration in college. A few years ago they gave
me a year of retraining so I could handle long distance
displacement machinery. If you're really interested in
theory, you ought to ask someone at Cape Kennedy.
Here we are."

Two escalators, one going up, one motionless. They
rode up. Jerryberry asked, "Why didn't they build closer?
Think of all the walking we'd save."

"You never heard a 707 taking off?"

"No."

"Sound is only part of it. If a plane ever crashed
here, nobody would want it hitting all the main buildings
at once."

The escalator led to two semicircular chambers. One
was empty but for a maze of chairs and couches and
low partitions, all done in old chrome and fading orange.
In the other, the couches had been ripped out and replaced with instrument consoles. Jerryberry counted half
a dozen men supervising the displays.

A dim snoring sound began somewhere, like an electric
razor going in the next door apartment. Jerryberry turned
his head, seeking. It was outside. Outside, behind a wall
of windows, a tiny single-engine plane taxied down a
runway.

"Yes, we still function as an airport," said Nils Kjerulf. "Skydiving, sport flying, gliding. I fly some myself. The jumbo jet pilots used to hate us; we use up just as much landing time as a 747. Now we've got the runways to ourselves."

"I gather you were a manager somewhere—"

"Right here. I ran this terminal before anyone had heard of teleportation. I watched it ruin us. Thirty years, Mr. Jansen."

"With no offense intended whatever, why did they train a professional administrator in quantum displacement physics? Why not the other way around?"

"There *weren't* any experts where the long distance booths were concerned, Mr. Jansen. They're *new.*"

"What have you learned in two years? Do you still get many breakdowns?"

"We still do. Every two weeks or so, something goes out of synch. Then we go out of service for however long it takes to find it and fix it. Usually about an hour."

"And what happens to the passenger?"

Kjerulf looked surprised. "Nothing. He stays where he started—or rather, that giant neutrino we were talking about is reflected back to the transmitter if the receiver can't pick it up. The worst thing that can happen is that the link to the velocity damper could be lost, in which case—but we've developed safeguards against that.

"No, the passengers just stop coming in, and we go out of service, and the other companies take the overflow. There isn't any real competition between the companies any more. What's the point? TWA and United and Eastern and the rest used to advertise that they had better meals in flight, more comfortable seats, prettier hostesses . . . like that. How long do you *spend* in a displacement booth? So when we converted over, we set the dialing system up so you just dial Los Angeles International or whatever, and the companies get customers at random. Everyone saves a fortune in advertising."

"An anti-trust suit—"

"Would have us dead to rights. Nobody's done it, because there's no point. It works, the way we run it. Each company has its own velocity shift damper. We couldn't all get knocked out at once. In an emergency, I think any of the companies could handle all of the long distance traffic."

"Mr. Kjerulf, what is a velocity shift damper?"

Kjerulf looked startled. Jerryberry said, "I took journalism."

"Ah."

"It's not just curiosity. My dad lost a fortune on airline stock—"

"So did I," said Kjerulf, half-smiling with old pain.

"Oh?"

"Sometimes I feel I've sold out. The booths couldn't possibly compete with the airlines, could they? They wouldn't send far enough. Yet they ruined us."

"My dad figured the same way."

"And now the booths *do* send that far, and I'm working for them, or they're working for me. There wasn't all that much reason to build the long distance systems at airports. Lots of room here, of course, and an organization already set up . . . but they really did it to save the airline companies."

"A little late."

"Perhaps. Some day they'll turn us into a public utility." Kjerulf looked about the room, then called to a man seated near the flat wall of the semicircle. "Dan!"

"Yo!" the man boomed without looking up.

"Can you spare me twenty minutes for a public relations job?"

The man stood up, then climbed up on his chair. He looked slowly about the room. Jerryberry guessed that he could see every instrument board from where he was sitting. He called, "Sure, go. No sweat."

They took the cart back to the terminal. They entered a booth. Jerryberry inserted his CBA credit card, then waited while Kjerulf dialed.

They were in a concrete building. Beyond large square windows, a sunlit sea of blue water heaved and splashed, almost at floor level. Men looked around curiously, recognized Nils Kjerulf, turned back to their work.

"Lake Michigan. And out there—" Kjerulf pointed. Jerryberry saw a tremendous white mass, a flattened dome, very regular. A great softly rounded island. "—is the United Airlines velocity damper. All of the dampers look about like that, but they float in different lakes or oceans. Aeroflot uses the Caspian Sea. The TWA damper is in the Gulf of Mexico."

"Just what is it?"

"Essentially it's a hell of a lot of soft iron surrounded by a hell of a lot more foam plastic, enough to float it, plus a displacement booth receiver feeding into the iron. Look, see it surge?"

The island rose several feet, slowly, then fell back as slowly. Ripples moved outward, became waves as they reached the station.

"That must have been a big load. Now, here's how it works. You know that the rotation of the Earth puts a limit on how far you can send a load. If you were to shift from here to Rio de Janiero, say, you'd flick in moving up and sideways; mainly up, because Rio and LA are almost the same distance from the equator.

"But with the long distance booths, the receiver picks up the kinetic energy and shunts it to the United Air Lines velocity damper. That big mass of iron surges up or down or sideways until the water stops it—or someone flicks in from Rio and the damping body stops cold."

Jerryberry thought about it. "What about conservation of rotation? It sounds like you're slowing down the Earth."

"We are. There's nothing sacred about conservation of

126

rotation, except that the energy has to go somewhere. There are pumps to send water through the damper bodies if they get too hot."

Jerryberry pulled out the Minox. "Mind if I take some pictures?"

"No, go ahead."

The Minox was a movie camera, but it would not have the resolution of a press camera. No matter. If he had the time he could come back . . . not that he thought he would. He took shots of the men at work in the station, of Nils Kjerulf with his back to the windows. He shot almost a minute of the great white island itself. He was hoping it would surge; and presently it did, sinking sideways, surging up again. Waves beat at the station. A jet of white steam sprayed from the top of the great white mass.

"Good," he said briskly, to himself. He folded the spidery tripod legs and dropped the camera in his pocket. He turned to Kjerulf, who had been watching the proceedings with some amusement. "Mr. Kjerulf, can you tell me anything about traffic control? Is there any?"

"How do you mean? Customs?"

"Not exactly . . . but tell me about customs."

"The customs terminal in Los Angeles is at TWA. You haven't been out of the country recently? No? Well, any big city airport has a customs terminal. In a small country there's likely to be just one. If you dial a number outside the country, *any* country, you wind up in somebody's customs terminal. The booths there don't have dials, you see. You have to cross the customs line to dial out."

"Clever. Are there any restrictions on traffic within the United States?"

"No, you just drop your chocolate dollars in and dial. Unless it's a police matter. If the police know that someone's trying to leave the city, they may set up a watch in the terminals. We can put a delay on the terminals, to give a detective time to look at a passenger's face and see if he's who they want."

"But nothing to stop passengers from coming in."

"No, except that it's possible to . . ." Kjerulf trailed off oddly, then finished, ". . . turn off any booth by remote control, from the nearest JumpShift maintenance system. What are you thinking of, the Mall Riot?"

"Yah."

There was no more to say. He left Nils Kjerulf in the United terminal in Los Angeles. He dialed for Customs.

For several minutes Jerryberry watched them flicking in. There were two types:

The tourists came in couples, sometimes with a child or two. They flicked in looking interested and harried and a little frightened. Their clothing was outlandish and extraordinary. Before they left the booths they would look about them mistrustfully. Sometimes they formed larger groups.

The businessmen traveled alone. They wore conservative or old fashioned clothing and carried one suitcase: large or small, but one. They were older than the tourists. They moved with authority, walking straight out of the booths the moment they appeared.

At the barrier: four men in identical dark suits with shield-shaped shoulder patches. Jerryberry was on the wrong side of the barrier to command their attention. He was thinking of dialing himself to Mexico and back . . . when one of them noticed him and pegged him as a newstaper.

His name was Gregory Scheffer. Small and round and middle-aged, he perched on the wooden barrier and clasped one knee in both hands. "Sure, I can talk awhile. This isn't one of the busy days. The only time these booths really get a workout is Christmas and New Year and Bastille Day and like that. Look around you," he said, waving a pudgy hand expansively. "About four times as many incoming as there was six months ago. I used to want to search every bag that came through, just to be doing something. If we keep getting more and more of them this way, we'll need twice as many customs people next year."

"Why do you suppose—"

"Did you know that the long distance booths have been operating for *two solid years?* It's only in the last six months or so that we've started to get so many passengers. They had to get used to traveling again. Look around you, look at all this space. It used to be *full,* before JumpShift came along. People have got out of the habit of traveling, that's all there is to it. For twenty solid years. They have to get back into it."

"Guess so." Jerryberry tried to remember why he was here. "Mr. Scheffer—"

"Greg."

"Jerryberry. Customs' main job is to stop smuggling, isn't it?"

"Well . . . it used to be. Now we only slow it down, and not very damn much. Nobody in his right mind would smuggle anything through customs. There are safer ways."

"Oh?"

"Diamonds, for instance. Diamonds are practically indestructible. You could rig a cargo booth in Kansas to receive from . . . oh, there's a point in the South Pacific to match anyplace in the United States: same longitude, opposite latitude. You don't need a velocity damper if you put the boat in the right place. Diamonds? You could ship in Swiss watches that way. Though that's pretty finicky. You'd want to pad them."

"Good grief. You could smuggle anything you pleased, anywhere."

"Just about. You don't need the ocean trick. Say you rig a booth a mile south of the Canadian border, and another booth a mile north. That's not much of a jump. You can flick further than that just in LA. I think we're obsolete," said Scheffer. "I think smuggling laws are obsolete. You won't publish this?"

"I won't use your name."

". . . I guess that's okay."

"Can you get me over to the incoming booths? I want to take some pictures."

"What for?"

"I'm not sure yet."

"Let's see some ID." Gregory Scheffer didn't trust evasive answers. The incoming booths were in his jurisdiction. He studied the CBA card for a few seconds, suddenly said, "Jansen! Mall Riot!"

"Right."

"What was it like?"

Jerryberry invested half a minute telling him. "So now I'm trying to find out how it got started. If there were some way to stop all of those people from pouring in like that . . ."

"You won't find it here. Look, a dozen passengers and we're almost busy. A thousand people suddenly pour through those booths and what would we do? Hide under something, that's what we'd do."

"I still want to see the incoming booths."

Scheffer thought it over, shrugged, and let him through. He stood at Jerryberry's shoulder while Jerryberry used his eye and his camera.

The booth was just like a street corner booth, except for the blank metal face where a dial would be. "I don't know what's underneath," Scheffer told him. "For all of me, it's just like any other booth. How much work would it be to leave off the dial?"

Which made sense. But it was no help at all.

VI

They tape the *Tonight Show* at two in the afternoon.

Twenty minutes into it, the first guest is lolling at his ease, just rapping, talking off the top of his head, ignoring the probable hundred million eyes behind the cameras. This is a valuable knack, and rare. *Tonight's* first guest is a series hero in a science fiction tapezine.

He is saying, "Have you ever seen a red tide? It's *thick* down at Hermosa Beach. I was there this weekend. In the daytime it's just dirty water, muddy-looking, and it smells. But at *night*—"

This enthusiasm that can reach through a TV screen to touch fifty million minds, this enthusiasm is in no way artificial. He means it. He only expresses it better than most men. He leans forward in his chair; his eyes blaze; there is harsh tension in his voice. "The breakers glow like churning blue fire! Those plankton are fluorescent. And they're all through the wet sand. Walk across it, it flashes blue light under your feet! Kick it, scuff your feet through it, it lights up. Throw a handful of sand, it flashes where it hits! The light isn't just on the surface. Stamp your foot, you can see the structure of the sand by the way it flares. You've got to see it to believe it," he says.

They will run the tape starting at eight-thirty tonight.

VII

Standard booths: how standardized?
Who makes them besides JumpShift? Monopoly? How extensive?
Skip spaceflight?

Space exploration depended utterly on teleportation.

131

But the subject was likely to be very technical and not very useful. He could gain time by skipping it entirely, Jerryberry considered, then turned the question mark into an exclamation point.

His twelve hours had become nine.

Of the half dozen key clubs to which he belonged, the Cave des Roys was the quietest. A place of stone and wood, a good place to sit and think. The wall behind the bar was several hundred wine bottles in a cement matrix. Jerryberry looked into the strange lights in the glass, sipped occasionally at a silver fizz, jotted down whatever occurred to him.

Sociology. What has teleportation done to society?
Cars.
Oil companies. Oil stocks. See back issues Wall Street Journal. *Watts Riot? Chicago Riot?* He crossed that last one out. The Chicago Riot had been political, hadn't it? Then he couldn't remember any other riots. They were too far in the past. He wrote:
Riot control. Police procedure.
Crime? The crime rate should have soared after displacement booths provided the instant getaway. Had it?

Sooner or later he was going to have to drop in at police headquarters. He'd hate that, but he might learn something. Likewise the library, for several hours of dull research. Then?

He certainly wasn't going to persuade everybody to give up displacement booths.

He wrote, *OBJECTIVE: Demonstrate that displacement booths imply instant riot. It's a social problem. Solve it on that basis.* For the sake of honesty he added, *Get 'em off my back. CROWDS.* In minutes the Mall had become a milling mass of men. But he'd seen crowds form almost as fast. It might happen regularly in certain places. After a moment's thought he wrote: *Tahiti. Jerusalem. Mecca. Easter Island. Stonehenge. Olduvai Gorge.*

He stood up. Start with the phone calls.

"Doctor Robin Whyte," Jerryberry said to the phone screen. "Please."

The receptionist at Seven Sixes was no sex symbol. She was old enough to be Jerryberry's aunt, and handsome rather than beautiful. She heard him out with a noncommittal dignity that, he sensed, could turn glacial in an instant.

"Barry Jerome Jansen," he said carefully.

He waited on HOLD, watching dark red patterns flow upward in the phone screen.

Key clubs were neither new nor rare. Some were small and local; others were chains, existing in a dozen or a hundred locations. Everyone belonged to a club; most people belonged to several.

But Seven Sixes was something else. Its telephone number was known universally. Its membership, large in absolute terms, was small for an organization so world wide. It included presidents, kings, winners of various brands of Nobel prize. Its location was—unknown. Somewhere in Earth's temperate zones. Jerryberry had never heard of its displacement booth number being leaked to anyone.

It took a special kind of gall for one of Jerryberry's social standing to dial 666-6666. He had learned that gall in journalism class. *Go to the source*—no matter how highly placed; be polite, be prepared to wait, but keep trying, and never, never worry about wasting the great man's time.

Funny: they still called it journalism, though newspapers had died. And the Constitution that had protected newspapers still protected "the Press". For awhile. But laws could change . . .

The screen cleared.

Robin Whyte the physicist had been a mature man of formidable reputation, back when JumpShift first demonstrated teleportation. Today, twenty-five years later, he was the last living member of the team that had formed JumpShift. His scalp was pink and bare. His face was round and soft, almost without wrinkles, but slack, as if the muscles were tired. He looked like somebody's favorite grandfather.

He looked Jerryberry Jansen up and down, very thoroughly. He said, "I wanted to see what you looked like." He reached for the cutoff switch.

"I didn't do it," Jerryberry said quickly.

Whtye stopped with his finger on the cutoff. "No?"

"I am not responsible for the Mall Riot. I hope to prove it."

The old man thought it over. "And you propose to involve *me*? How?"

Jerryberry took a chance. "I think I can demonstrate that displacement booths and the Mall Riot are intimately connected. My problem is that I don't know enough about displacement booth technology."

"And you want *my* help?"

"You invented the displacement booths practically single-handed," Jerryberry said straightfaced. "Instant riots, instant getaways, instant smuggling. Are you going to just walk away from the problem?"

Robin Whyte laughed in a high-pitched voice, his head thrown way back, his teeth white and perfect and clearly false. Jerryberry waited, wondering if it would work.

"All right," Whyte said. "Come on over. Wait a minute, what am I thinking? *You* can't come to Seven Sixes. I'll meet your somewhere. *L'Orangerie*, New York City. At the bar."

The screen cleared before Jerryberry could answer. *That was quick*, he thought. And, *Move, idiot. Get there before he changes his mind.*

In New York it was just approaching cocktail hour. *L'Orangerie* was polished wood and dim lighting, and chafing dishes of Swedish meatballs on toothpicks. Jerryberry captured a few to go with his drink. He had not had lunch yet.

Robin Whyte wore a long sleeved grey one-piece with a collar that drapped into a short cape; and the cape was all the shifting rainbow colors of an oil film. The height of fashion, except that it should have been skin tight. It was loose all over, bagging where Whyte bagged, and it looked very comfortable. Whyte sipped at a glass of milk.

"One by one I give up my sins," he said. "Drinking was the last, and I haven't really turned loose of it yet. But almost. That's why your reverse salesmanship hooked me in. I'll talk to anyone. What do I call you?"

"Barry Jerome Jansen."

"Let me put it this way. I'm Robbie. What do I call you?"

"Oh. Jerryberry."

Whyte laughed. "I can't call anyone Jerryberry. Make it Barry."

"God bless you, sir."

"What do you want to know?"

"How big is JumpShift?"

"Ooohhh, pretty big. What's your standard of measurement?"

Jerryberry, who had wondered if he was being laughed at, stopped wondering. "How many kinds of booth do you make?"

"Hard to say. Three, for general use. Maybe a dozen more for the space industry. Those are still experimental. We lose money on the space industry. We'd make it back if we could start producing drop ships in quantity. We've got a ship on the drawing boards that would transmit itself to any drop ship receiver."

Jerryberry prompted him. "And three for general use, you said."

"Yes. We've made over three hundred million passenger booths in the past twenty years. Then there's a general use cargo booth. The third model is a tremendous portable booth for shipping really big, fragile cargoes. Like a prefab house, or a rocket booster, or a live sperm whale. You can set the thing in place almost anywhere, using three strap-on helicopter setups. I didn't believe it when I saw it." Whyte sipped at his milk. "You've got to remember that I'm not in the business any more. I'm still Chairman of the Board, but a bunch of younger people give most of the orders, and I hardly ever get into the factories."

"Does JumpShift have a monopoly on displacement booths?"

He saw the *Newstaper!* reaction, a tightening at Whyte's eyes and lips. "Wrong word," he said quickly. "Sorry. What I meant was, who makes displacement booths? I'm sure you make most of the passenger booths in the United States."

"All of them. It's not a question of monopoly. Anyone could make his own booths. Any community could. But it would be hideously expensive. The cost doesn't drop until you're making millions of them. So suppose . . . Chile, for instance. Chile has less than a million passenger booths, all JumpShift model. Suppose they *had* gone ahead and made their own. They'd have only their own network, unless they built a direct copy of some other model. All the booths in a network have to have the same volume."

"Naturally."

"In practice there are about ten networks, world wide. The USSR network is the biggest by far. I think the smallest is Brazil—"

"What happens to the air in a receiver?"

Whyte burst out laughing. "I *knew* that was coming! It never fails." He sobered. "We tried a lot of things. It turns out the only practical solution is to send the air in the receiver back to the transmitter, which means that every transmitter has to be a receiver too."

"Then you could get a free ride if you knew who was about to flick in from where, when."

"Of course you could, but would you want to bet on it?"

"I might, if I had something to smuggle past Customs."

"How do you mean?"

"I'm just playing with ideas. The incoming booths at Customs are incoming because there's no way to dial out—"

"I remember. Type I's with the dials removed."

"Okay. Say you wanted to smuggle something into the country. You flick to Customs in Argentina. Then a friend flicks from California to Argentina, into your booth. You wind up in his booth, in California, and *not* behind the Customs barrier."

"Brilliant," said Whyte. "Unfortunately there's a failsafe to stop anyone from flicking into an occupied booth."

"Damn."

"Sorry," Whyte said grinning. "What do you care? There are easier ways to smuggle. Too many. I'm not really sorry. I'm a *laissez-faire* man myself."

"I wondered if you could do something with dials, to stop another Mall Riot."

Whyte thought about it. "Not by taking the dials off. If you wanted to stop a riot you'd have to stop people from coming *in*. Counters on the booths, maybe."

"Mmm."

"What was it like, Barry?"

"Crowded. Like a dam broke. The law did shut the booths down from outside, but not fast enough. Maybe that's the answer. Cut out the booths at the first sign of trouble."

"We'd get a lot of people mad at us."

"You would, wouldn't you?"

"Like the power brownouts in the '70s and '80s. Or like obscene telephone calls. You couldn't do anything about them, except get more and more uptight . . . readier to smash things . . . that's why riots happen, Barry. People who are a little bit angry all the time."

"Oh?"

"All the riots I remember." Whyte smiled. "There haven't been any for a long time. Give JumpShift some credit for that. We stopped some of the things that kept everyone a little bit angry all the time. Smog. Traffic jams. Slow mail. Slum landlords; you don't *have* to live near your job or your welfare office or whatever. Job hunting. Crowding. Have you ever been in a traffic jam?"

"Maybe when I was a little boy."

"Friend of mine was a college professor for awhile. His problem was he lived in the wrong place. Five days a week, he would spend an hour driving to work—you don't believe me?—and an hour and a quarter driving home, because traffic was heavier then. Eventually he gave it up to be a writer."

"Gawd, I should hope so!"

"It wasn't even that rare," Whyte said seriously. "It was rough if you owned a car, and rougher if you didn't. JumpShift didn't *cause* riots, we *cured* them."

And he seemed to wait for Jerryberry's agreement.

Silence stretched long enough to become embarrassing . . . yet the only thing Jerryberry might have said to break it was, "But what about the Mall Riot?" He held his peace.

"Drain that thing," Whyte said abruptly. "I'll *show* you."

"Show me?"

"Finish that drink. We're going places." Whyte drank half a glass of milk in three gulps, his Adam's apple bobbing. He lowered the glass. "Well?"

"Ready."

On Madison Avenue the sunset shadows ran almost horizontally along the glass faces of buildings. Robin Whyte stepped out of *L'Orangerie,* turned right. Four feet away, a displacement booth.

In the booth he blocked the hand Jerryberry would have used to insert his CBA card. "My treat. This was my idea . . . anyway, some of these numbers are secret." He inserted his own card, and dialed three numbers.

Twice they saw rows of long distance booths. Then it was bright sunlight and sea breeze. Far out beyond a sandy beach and white waves, a great cylinder with a rounded top rose high out of the water. Orange letters on the curved metal flank read:

JUMPSHIFT FRESH WATER TRANSPORT

"I could take you out in a boat," said Whyte. "But it would be a waste of time. You wouldn't see much. Nothing but vacuum inside. You know how it works?"

"Sure."

"Teleportation was like laser technology. One big breakthrough, and then a thousand ways to follow up on it. We spent *twelve solid years* building continuous teleport pumps for various municipalities, to ship fresh water in various directions. When all the time the real problem was *getting* the fresh water, not moving it.

"Do you know how we developed this gimmick? My secretary dreamed it up one night at an office party. She was about half smashed, but she wrote it down, and the next morning we all took turns trying to read her handwriting . . . well, never mind. It's a simple idea. You build a tank more than thirty-four feet above sea level, open at the bottom, airtight, and you put the teleport pump in the top. You teleport the air out. When the air goes the seawater boils. From then on you're teleporting cold water vapor. It condenses wherever you ship it, and you get fresh water. Want to take pictures?"

"No."

"Then let's look at the results," Whyte said, and dialed.

Now it was even brighter. The booth was backed up against a long wooden building. Far away was a white glare of salt flats, backed by blue ghosts of mountains. Jerryberry blinked, squinted. Whyte opened the door.

Jerryberry said, "Whoooff!"

"Death Valley. Hot, isn't it?"

"Words fail me at a time like this; but I suggest you look up the dictionary definition of *blast furnace*." Jerryberry felt perspiration start as a rippling itch all over him. "I'm going to pretend I'm in a sauna. Why doesn't anyone ever put displacement booths inside?"

"They did for awhile. There were too many burglaries. Let's go around back."

They walked around the dry wooden building . . .

. . . and into an oasis. Jerryberry was jarred. On one side of the building, the austere beauty of a barren desert. On the other was a manicured forest: rows and rows of trees.

"We can grow damn near anything out here. We started with date palms, went to orange and grapefruit trees, pineapples, a *lot* of rice paddies, mangoes—anything that grows in tropic climates will grow here, as long as you give it enough water."

Jerryberry had already noticed the water tower. It looked just like the transmitter. He said, "And the right soil."

"Well, yes. Soil isn't that good in Death Valley. We have to haul in too much fertilizer." Rivulets of perspiration ran down Whyte's cheeks. His soft face looked almost stern. "But the principle holds. With teleportation men can live practically anywhere. We gave people room. A man can work in Manhattan or Central Los Angeles or Central Anywhere and live in, in—"

"Nevada."

"Or Hawaii! Or the Grand Canyon! Crowding caused riots. We've eliminated crowding—for awhile, anyway.

At the rate we're going we'll still wind up shoulder to shoulder, but not until you and I are both dead."

Jerryberry considered keeping his mouth shut, decided he didn't have the will power. "What about pollution?"

"What?"

"Death Valley used to have an ecology as unique as its climate. What's your unlimited water doing to that?"

". . . Ruining it, I guess."

"Hawaii, you said. Grand Canyon. There are laws against putting up apartment buildings in national monuments, thank God. Hawaii probably has the population density of New York by now. Your displacement booths can put men anywhere, right? Even places they don't belong."

"Well, maybe they can," Whyte said slowly. "Pollution. Hmm. What do you know about Death Valley?"

"It's hot." Jerryberry was wet through.

"Death Valley used to be an inland sea. A salt sea. Then the climate changed and all the water went away. What did *that* do to the ecology?"

Jerryberry scratched his head. "A *sea?*"

"Yes, a sea! And drying it up ruined one ecology and started another, just like we're doing. But never mind that. I want to show you some things. Pollution, huh?" Whyte's grip on Jerryberry's arm was stronger than it had any right to be.

Whyte was angry. In the booth he froze with his brow furrowed and his forefinger extended. Trying to remember a number. Then he dialed in trembling haste.

He dialed two sequences. Jerryberry saw the interior of an airline terminal, then—dark.

"Oh, damn. I forgot it would be night here."

"Where are we?"

"Sahara Desert. Rudolph Hill Reclamation Project. No, don't go out there, there's nothing to see at night. Do you know anything about the project?"

"You're trying to grow a forest in the middle of the Sahara. Trees, leaf eating molds, animals, the whole ecology." Jerryberry tried to see out through the glass. Nothing. "How's it working?"

"Well enough. If we can keep it going another thirty years, this part of the Sahara should stay a forest. Do you think we're wiping out another ecology?"

"Well, it's probably *worth* it *here . . .*"

"The Sahara used to be a lush, green land. It was men who turned it into a desert, over thousands of years, mainly through overgrazing. We're trying to put it back."

"Okay," said Jerryberry. He heard Whyte dialing. Through the glass he could now see stars, and a horizon etched with treetop shadows.

He squinted against airport terminal lights. He asked, "How did we get through Customs?"

"Oh, the Hill Project is officially United States territory." Whyte swung the local directory out from the wall, leafed through it before dialing a second time. "Some day you'll make *any* journey by dialing two numbers," he was saying. "Why should you have to dial your local airport first? Just dial a long distance booth near your destination. Of course the changeover will cost us considerable. Here we are."

Bright sunlight, sandy beach, blue sea stretching to infinity. The booth was backed up against a seaside hotel. Jerryberry followed Whyte, whose careful, determined stride took him straight toward the water.

They stopped at the edge. Tiny waves brushed just to the tips of their shoes.

"Carpinteria. They advertise this beach as the safest beach in the world. It's also the dullest, of course. No waves. Remember anything about Carpinteria, Barry?"

"I don't think so."

"Oil slick disaster. A tanker broke up out there, opposite Santa Barbara, which is up the coast a little. All of these beaches were black with oil. I was one of the volunteers working here to save the birds, to get the oil off their feathers. They died anyway. Almost fifty years ago, Barry."

Part of a history lesson floated to the top of his mind. "I thought that happened in England."

"There were several oil slick disasters. Almost I might say, there were many. These days we ship oil by displacement booths. And we don't use anything like as *much* oil."

"No cars."

"No oil wells, practically."

They shifted.

From an underwater dome they gazed out at an artificial reef made from old car bodies. The shapes seemed to blend, their outlines obscured by mud and time and swarming fish. Bent and twisted metal bodies had long since rusted away, but their outlines remained, held by shellfish living and dead. Ghosts of cars, the dashboards and upholstery showing through. An occasional fiberglass wreck showed as if it had been placed yesterday.

The reef went on and on, disappearing into grey distance.

All those cars.

"People used to joke about the East River catching fire and burning to the ground. It was that dirty," said Whyte. "Now look at it."

Things floated by. Wide patches of scum, with plastic and metal objects embedded in them. Jerryberry said, "It's pretty grubby."

"Maybe, but it's not an open sewer. Teleportation made it easier to get rid of garbage."

"I guess my trouble is, I never saw anything as dirty as you claim it was. Oil slicks. Lake Michigan. The Mississippi." *Maybe you're exaggerating.* "Just what has tele-portation done for garbage collection?"

"There are records. Pictures."

"But even with your wonderful bottomless garbage cans, it must be easier just to dump it in the river."

"Ahh, I guess so."

"And you still have to *put* the gupp somewhere after you collect it."

Whyte was looking at him oddly. "Very shrewd, Barry. Let me show you the next step."

Whyte kept his hand covered as he dialed. "Secret," he said. "JumpShift experimental laboratory. We don't need a lot of room, because experiments with teleportation aren't particularly dangerous . . ."

. . . but there was room, lots of it. The building was a huge inflated Quonset hut. Through the transparent panels Jerryberry could see other buildings, set wide apart on bare dirt. The sun was 45° up. If he had known which way was north he could have guessed longitude and latitude.

A very tall, very black woman in a lab smock greeted Whyte with glad cries. Whyte introduced her as "Gemini Jones, Phud. Gem, where do you handle disposal of radio-active waste?"

"Building Four." The physicist's hair exploded around her head like a black dandelion, adding unnecessary inches to her height. She looked down at Jerryberry with genial curiosity. "Newstaper?"

"Yah."

"Don't ever try to fool anyone. The eyes give you away."

They took the booth to Building Four. Presently they were looking down through several densities of leaded glass into a cylindrical metal chamber.

"We get a package every twenty minutes or so," said

Gem Jones. "There's a transmitter linked to this receiver in every major power plant in the United States. We keep the receiver on all the time. If a package gets reflected back, we have to find out what's wrong, and that can get hairy, because it's usually wrong at the drop ship."

Jerryberry said, "Drop ship?"

Gemini Jones showed surprise at his ignorance. Whyte said, "Back up a bit, Barry. What's the most dangerous garbage ever?"

"Give me a hint."

"Radioactive wastes from nuclear power plants. Most dangerous per pound, anyway. They send those wastes here, and we send them to a drop ship. You've *got* to know what a drop ship is."

"Of *course* I—"

"A drop ship is a moving teleport receiver with one end open. Generally it's attached to a space probe. The payload flicks in with a velocity different from that of the drop ship. Of course it's supposed to come tearing out the open end, which means somebody has to keep it turned right. And of course the drop ship only operates in vacuum."

"Package," Gem Jones said softly. Something had appeared in the metal chamber below. It was gone before Jerryberry could quite see what it was.

"Just where is your drop ship?"

"Circling Venus," said Whyte. "Originally it was part of the second Venus expedition. You can send anything through a drop ship: fuel, oxygen, food, water, even small vehicles. There are drop ships circling every planet in the solar system, except Neptune.

"When the Venus expedition came home they left the drop ship in orbit. We thought at first that we might send another expedition through it, but—face it, Venus just isn't worth it. We're using the planet as a garbage dump, which is about all it's good for.

"Now, there's no theoretical reason we can't send unlimited garbage through the Venus drop ship, as long as we keep the drop ship oriented right. Many transmitters, one receiver. The payload doesn't stay in the receiver more than a fraction of a second. If it did get overloaded, why, some of the garbage would be reflected back to the transmitter and we'd send it again. No problem."

"What about cost?"

"Stupendous. Horrible. Too high for any kind of garbage less dangerous than this radioactive stuff. But maybe we can bring it down someday." Whyte stopped; he looked puzzled. "Mind if I sit down?"

There were fold-up chairs around a card table with empty pop bulbs on it. Whyte sat down rather disturbingly hard, even with Gem Jones trying to support his weight. She asked, "Can I get Doctor Janesko?"

"No, Gem, just tired. Is there a pop machine—?"

Jerryberry had found the pop machine. He paid a chocolate dollar for a clear plastic bulb of cola. He turned, and almost bumped into Gemini Jones.

She spoke low, but there was harsh intensity in her voice. "You're running him ragged. Will you lay off of him?"

"He's been running *me!*" Jerryberry whispered.

"I believe it. Well, don't let him run you so fast. Remember, he's an old man."

Whyte pulled the cola bulb open and drank. "Better," he sighed . . . and was back in high gear. "Now, you see? We're *cleaning up* the world. *We* aren't polluters."

"Right."

"Thank you."

"I never should have raised the subject. What have you got for the Mall Riot?"

Whyte looked confused.

"The Mall Riot is still going on, and they're still blaming me."

"And you still blame JumpShift."

"It's a matter of access," Jerryberry said patiently.

"Even if only . . . ten men in a million, say, would loot a store, given the opportunity, that's still about four thousand people in the United States. And all four thousand can get to the Santa Monica Mall in the time it takes to dial twenty-one digits."

When Whyte spoke again he sounded bitter. "What are we supposed to do, stop inventing things?"

"No, of course not." Jerryberry pulled open another bulb of cola.

"What, then?"

"I don't know. Just . . . keep working things out." He drank. "There's always another problem behind the one you just solved. Does that mean you should stop solving problems?"

"Well, let's solve this one."

They sat sipping cola. It was good to sit down. *The old man's running me ragged,* thought Jerryberry.

"Crowds," he said.

"Right."

"You can make one receiver for many transmitters. In fact . . . every booth in a city receives from any other booth. Can you make a booth that transmits only?"

Whyte looked up. "Sure. Give it an unlisted number. Potentially it would still be a receiver, of course."

"Because you have to flick the air back to the transmitter."

"How's this sound? You put an E on the booth number. The only dials with E's in them are at police stations and fire stations. E for Emergency."

"All *right*. Now you put a lot of these escape booths wherever a crowd might gather—"

"That could be anywhere. You said so yourself."

". . . Yah."

"We'd have to double the number of booths in the country . . . or cut the number of incoming booths in half. You'd have to walk twice as far to get where you're going from any given booth. Would it be worth it?"

"I don't think this is the last riot," said Jerryberry. "It's growing. Like tourism. Your short hop booths cut tourism way down. The long distance booths are bringing it back, but slowly. Would you believe a permanent floating riot? A mob that travels from crowd to crowd, carrying coin purses, looting where they can . . ."

"I *hate* that idea."

Jerryberry put his hand on the old man's shoulder. "Don't worry about it. You're a hero. You made a miracle. What people do with it isn't your fault. Maybe you even saved the world. The pollution was getting very rough before JumpShift came along."

"By God, it was."

"I've got to be going. There are things I want to see before I run out of time."

VIII

Tahiti. Jerusalem. Mecca. Easter Island. Stonehenge. The famous places of the world. Places a man might dial almost on impulse. Names that came unbidden to the mind.

Mecca. Vast numbers of Muslims (a number he could look up later) bowed toward Mecca five times a day. The Koran called for every Muslim to make a pilgrimage to Mecca at least once in a lifetime. The city's only industry was the making of religious articles. And you could get there just by dialing . . .

Jerusalem. Sacred to three major religions. Jews still toasted each other at Passover: "Next year in Jerusalem." Still a forming ground of history, after thousands of years. And you could get there just by dialing . . .

Stonehenge. An ancient mystery. What race erected those stones, and when, and why? These would never be known with certainty. From the avenue at the northeast entrance, a path forked and ran up a hill between burial mounds . . . and there was a long distance displacement booth on the hill.

It would be eleven at night in Stonehenge. One in the morning in Mecca and Jerusalem. No action there. Jerryberry crossed them out.

Eiffel Tower, the Pyramids, the Sphinx, the Vatican; dammit, the most memorable places on Earth were all in the same general area. What could he see at midnight?

Well—

Tahiti. Say "tropical paradise" and every stranger in earshot will murmur, "Tahiti." Once Hawaii had had the same reputation; but Hawaii was too close to civilization. Hawaii had been civilized. Tahiti, isolated in the southern hemisphere, might have escaped that fate.

Everything lurched as he finished dialing. Jerryberry stumbled against the booth wall. Briefly he was terrified. But he'd be dead if the velocity transfer had failed. It must be a little out of synch.

He knew too much, that was all.

There were six booths of different makes, this side of Customs. The single official had a hopeless look. He waved through a constant stream of passengers without seeming to see them.

Jerryberry moved with the stream.

They were mostly men. Many had cameras; few had luggage. English, American, French, German, some Spanish and USSR. Most were dressed lightly—and poorly, in cheap clothes ready to come apart. They swarmed toward the outgoing booths, the rectangular Common Market booths with one glass side. Jerryberry saw unease and dismay on many faces. Perhaps it was the new, clean modern building that bothered them. This was an island paradise? Air conditioning. Fluorescent lighting.

Jerryberry stood in line for the phone. Then he found that it wouldn't take his coins or his credit card. On his way to the change counter he thought to examine the displacement booths. They took only French money. He bought a heavy double handful of coins, then got back in line for the phone.

They have to get used to traveling again. Right on.

The computerized directory spoke English. He used it to get a string of booth numbers in downtown Papeete.

He was a roving newstaper again. Dial, watch the scene flick over, look around while inserting a coin and dialing. The coin slot was in the wrong place and the coins felt wrong, too big, too thin; and the dial was a disc with holes in it. A little practice had him in the routine.

There was beach front lined with partly built hotels in crazily original shapes. Of all the crowds he saw in Papeete, the thickest were on the beaches and in the water. Later he could not remember the color of the sand; he hadn't seen enough of it.

Downtown he found huge blocks of buildings faced in glass, some completed, some half built. He found old slums, and old mansions. But wherever the streets ran, past mansions or slums or new skyscrapers, he found tents and lean-tos and board shacks hastily nailed together. They filled the streets, leaving small clear areas around displacement booths and public rest rooms and far more basic portable toilets. An open-air market ran for several blocks, and was closed at both ends by crowds of tents. The only way in or out was by booth.

They're ahead of us, thought Jerryberry. *When you've got booths, who needs streets?* He was not amused. He was appalled.

There were beggars. At first he was moving too fast; he didn't realize what they were doing. But wherever he flicked in, one or two habitants immediately came toward his booth. He stopped under a vertical glass cliff of a building, where the tents of the squatters ran just to the bottom-most of a flight of stone steps, and waited.

Beggars. Some were natives, men and women and children, uniform in their dark bronze color and in their dress and their speech and the way they moved. They were a thin minority. Most were men, and white, and foreign. They came with their hands out, mournful or smiling; they spoke rapidly in what they guessed to be his language and were right about half the time.

He tried several other numbers. They were everywhere. Tahiti was a white man's daydream.

Suddenly he'd had enough. On his list of jotted numbers was one that would take him out of the city. Jerryberry dialed it.

Air puffed out of the booth when he opened the door. Jerryberry opened his jaws wide to pop his ears.

The view! He was near the peak of a granite mountain. Other mountains marched away before him, and the valleys between were green and lush. Greens and yellows and white cloud, the blue-grey of distant peaks, and beyond everything else, the sea.

It was a bus terminal. An ancient Greyhound was just pulling out. The driver stopped alongside him and shouted something amiable in French. Jerryberry smiled and shook his head violently. The driver shrugged and pulled away.

This could not have been the original terminal. Before displacement booths it could only have been reached after hours of driving. In moving the terminal up here, the touring company had saved the best for first and last.

The bus had looked full. Business was good.

Jerryberry stood for a long time, drinking in the view. This was the beauty that had made Tahiti famous. It was good to know that Tahiti's population explosion had left something intact.

In good time he remembered that he was running on a time limit. He walked around to the ticket window.

The young man in the booth laid a paperback book face down. He smiled agreeably. "Yes?"

"Do you speak English?"

"Certainly." He wore a kind of uniform, but his features and color were those of a Tahitian. His English was good, the accent not quite French. "Would you like to buy a tour ticket?"

"No, thanks. I'd like to talk, if you have a minute."

"What would you like to talk about?"

"Tahiti. I'm a newstaper."

The man's smile drooped a bit. "And you wish to give us free publicity."

"Something like that."

The smile was gone. "You may return to your country and tell them that Tahiti is full."

"I noticed that. I have just come from Papeete."

"I have the honor to own a house in Papeete. A good property. We, my family and myself, we have been forced to move out! There was no, no passage—" he was too angry to talk as fast as he wanted. "No passage from the house to anyplace. We were surrounded by the tents of the—" He used a word Jerryberry did not recognize. "We could not buy an instant-motion booth for the house. I had not the money. We could not have moved the booth to the house because the—" That word again. "—blocked the streets. The police can do nothing. Nothing."

"Why not?"

"They are too many. We are not monsters; we cannot simply shoot them. It would be the only way to stop them. They come without money or clothing or a place to stay. And they are not the worst. You will tell them this when you return?"

"I'm recording," said Jerryberry.

"Tell them that the worst are those with much money, those who build hotels. They would turn our island into an enormous hotel! See!" He pointed where he could not have seen himself, down the slope of the mountain. "The Playboy Club builds a new hotel below us."

Jerryberry looked down to temporary buildings and a

great steel box with helicopter rotors on it. He filmed it on the Minox, then filmed a panoramic swoop of the mountains beyond, and finished with the scowling man in the ticket booth.

"Squatters," the ticket-taker said suddenly. "The word I wanted. The squatters are in my house now, I am sure of it, in my house since we moved out. Tell them we want no more squatters."

"I'll tell them," said Jerryberry.

Before he left he took one more long look about him. Green valleys, grey-blue mountains, distant line of sea . . . but his eyes kept dropping to the endless stream of supplies that poured from the Playboy Club's Type III cargo booth.

Easter Island. Tremendous, long-faced, solemn stone statues with topknots of red volcanic tuff. Cartoons of the statues were even more common than pictures ("Shut up until those archeologists leave," one statue whispers to another) and even pictures can only hint at their massive solemnity. But you could get there just by dialing . . .

Except that the directory wouldn't give him a booth number for Easter Island.

Surely there must be booth travel to Easter Island. Mustn't there? But how eager would the Peruvian government be to see a million tourists on Easter Island?

The other side of the coin. Displacement booths made any place infinitely accessible; but only if you moved a booth in. Jerryberry was grinning with delight as he dialed Los Angeles International. There *was* a defense.

IX

At the police station on Purdue Avenue he couldn't get anyone to talk to him.

The patience of a newstaper was unique in a world of instant transportation. He kept at it. Eventually a desk man stopped long enough to tell him, "Look, we don't have *time*. Everybody's out cleaning up the Mall Riot."

"Cleaning up? Is it over?"

"Just about. We had to move in old riot vehicles from Chicago. I guess we'll have to start building them again. But it's over."

"Good!"

"Too right. I don't mean to say we *got* them all. Some looters managed to jury-rig a cargo booth in the basement of Penney's. They moved their loot out that way, and then got out that way themselves. We're going to hate it the next time they show up. They've got guns now."

"A permanent floating riot?"

"Something like that. Look, I don't have time to talk." And he was back on the phone.

The next man Jerryberry stopped recognized him at once. "You're the man who started it all! Will you get out of my way?"

Jerryberry left.

Sunset on a summer evening. It was cocktail hour again . . . three and a half hours later.

Jerryberry felt unaccountably dizzy outside the police station. He rested against the wall. Too much change. Over and over again he had changed place and time and climate. From evening in New York to a humid seacoast to the dry furnace of Death Valley to night in the Sahara. It was hard to remember where he was. He had lost direction.

When he felt better he shifted to the Cave des Roys.

For each human being there is an optimum ratio between change and stasis. Too little change, he grows bored. Too little stability, he panics, loses his ability to adapt. One who marries six times in ten years will not change jobs. One who moves often to serve his company will maintain a stable marriage. A woman chained to one home and family may redecorate frantically, or take a lover, or go to many costume parties.

Displacement booths make novelty easy. Stability comes hard. For many the clubs were an element of stability. Many key clubs were chains; a man could leave his home in Wyoming and find his club again in Denver. Members tended to resemble one another. A man changing roles would change clubs.

Clubs were places to meet people, as buses and airports and even neighborhoods no longer were. Some clubs were good for pickups ("This card gets me laid"), others for heavy conversation. At the Beach Club you could always find a paddle tennis game.

The Cave was for quiet and stability. A quick drink and the cool darkness of the Cave's bar were just what Jerryberry needed. He looked into the lights in the wall of bottles and tried to remember a name. When it came he jotted it down, then finished his drink at leisure.

Harry McCord had been Police Chief in Los Angeles for twelve years; had been on the force for far longer. He had retired only last year. The computer-directory took some time to find him. He was living in Oregon.

He was living in a small house in the middle of a pine forest. From his porch Jerryberry could see the dirt road that joined him to civilization. It seemed to be fading away in weeds. But the displacement booth was new.

They drank beer on the porch. "Crime is a pretty general subject," said Harry McCord.

"Crime and displacement booths," said Jerryberry. "I want to know how your job was affected by the instant getaway."

"Ah."

Jerryberry waited.

"Pretty drastically, I guess. The booths came in . . . when? Nineteen ninety? But they came slowly. We had a chance to get used to them. Let's see, there were people who put displacement booths in their living rooms, and

155

when they got robbed they blamed us . . ," McCord talked, haltingly at first, gaining speed. He had always been something of a public figure. He talked well.

Burglary: The honors were even there. If the house or apartment had an alarm, the police could be on the scene almost instantly. If the burglar moved fast enough to get away he certainly wouldn't have time to rob his target.

There were sophisticated alarms now that would lock the displacement booth door from the inside. Often that held the burglar up just long enough for the police to shift in. At opposite extremes of professionalism, there were men who could get through an alarm system without setting it off—in which case there wasn't a hope in hell of catching them after they'd left—and men who had been caught robbing apartment houses because they'd forgotten to take coins for the booth in the lobby.

"Then there was Lon Willis. His MO was to prop the booth door open before he went to work on the house. If he set the alarm off he'd run next door and use that booth. Worked pretty well; it slowed us up just enough that we never did catch him. But one night he set off an alarm, and when he ran next door the next-door neighbor blew a small but adequate hole in him."

Murder: The alibi was an extinct species. A man attending a party in Hawaii could shoot a man in Paris in the time it would take him to use the bath room. "Like George Clayton Larkin did. Except that he used his credit card, and we got him," said McCord, "and we got Lucille Downey because she ran out of coins and had to ask at the magazine stand for change. With blood all over her sleeves!"

Pickpockets: "Do you have a lock pocket?"

"Sure," said Jerryberry. It was an inside pocket, lined with tough plastic. The zipper lock took two hands to open. "They're tough to get into, but not impossible."

"What's in it? Credit cards?"

"Right."

"And you can cancel them in three minutes. Picking pockets isn't profitable any more. If it was, they would have *mobbed* the Mall Riot."

Smuggling: Nobody even tried to stop it.

Drugs: "There's no way to keep them from getting in. Anyone who wants drugs can get them. We make arrests where we can, and so what? Me, I'm betting on Darwin."

"How do you mean?"

"The next generation won't use drugs because they'll be descended from people who had better sense. I'd legalize wireheading if it were up to me. With a wire in your pleasure center you're getting what all the drugs are supposed to give you, and no dope peddler can hold out on you."

Riots: The Mall Riot was the first *successful* riot in twenty years. "The police can get to a riot before it's a riot," said McCord. "We call them *flash crowds,* and we watch for them. We've been doing it ever since . . . well, ever since it became possible." He hesitated, evidently decided to go on. "See, the coin booths usually went into the shopping centers first and then the residential areas. It wasn't till JumpShift put them in the slum areas that we stopped having riots."

"Makes sense."

McCord laughed. "Even that's a half-truth. When the booths went into the slums, we pretty near stopped having slums. Everyone moved out. They'd commute."

"Why do you think the police didn't stop the Mall Riot?"

"That's a funny one, isn't it? I was there this afternoon. Did you get a chance to look at the cargo booth in Penney's basement?"

"No."

"It's a professional job. Whoever rigged it knew exactly what he was doing. No slips. He probably had a model to practice on. We traced it to a cargo receiver in downtown LA, but we don't know where it was sending to, because someone stayed behind and wrecked it and then skilled out. Real professional. Some gang has decided to make a profession of riots."

"You think this is their first job?"

"I'd guess. They must have seen the Mall type riots coming. Which is pretty shrewd, because a flash crowd couldn't have formed that fast before long distance displacement booths. It's a new crime. Makes me almost sorry I retired."

"How would you redesign the booths to make life easier for the police?"

But McCord wouldn't touch the subject. He didn't know anything about displacement booth design.

Seven o'clock. The interview with Evans was at ten.

Jerryberry shifted back to the Cave. He was beginning to get nervous. The Cave, and a good dinner, should help ease his stage fright.

He turned down a couple of invitations to join small groups. With the interview hanging over his head he'd be poor company. He sat alone, and continued to jot during dinner.

Escape booths. Send anywhere, receive only from police and fire departments.

Police can shut down all booths in an area. Except escape booths? No, that would let the looters escape too. But there might be no way to stop that. At least it would get the innocent bystanders out of a riot area.

Hah! *Escape booths send only to police station !!!*

He crossed that out and wrote, *All booths send only to police station! ! !* He crossed that out too and wrote an expanded version:

1) Riot signal from police station.

2) All booths in area stop receiving.

3) All booths in area send only to police station.

He went back to eating. Moments later he stopped with his fork half raised, put it down and wrote:

4) A million rioters stomp police station to rubble, from inside.

And it had seemed like such a good idea.

He was dawdling over coffee when the rest of it dropped into place. He went to a phone.

The secretary at Seven Sixes promised to have Dr. Whyte call as soon as he checked in. Jerryberry put a time limit on it, which seemed to please her.

McCord wasn't home.

Jerryberry went back to his coffee. He was feeling twitchy now. He had to know if this was possible. Otherwise he would be talking through his hat—in front of a big audience.

Twenty minutes later, as he was about to get up and call again, the headwaiter came to tell him that Dr. Robin Whyte was on the phone.

"It's a design problem," said Jerryberry. "Let me tell you how I'd like it to work, and then you can tell me if it's possible, okay?"

"Go ahead."

"First step is the police get word of a flash crowd, a Mall Riot type crowd. They throw emergency switches at Headquarters. Each switch affects the displacement booths in a small area."

"That's the way it works now."

"*Now* those switches *turn off* the booths. I'd like them to do something more complex. Set them so they can only receive from police and fire departments, and can only transmit to a police station."

"We can do that." Whyte half-closed his eyes to think. "Good. Then the police could release the innocent by-standers, send the injured to a hospital, hold the obvious

159

looters, get everybody's names . . . right. Brilliant. You'd put the receiver at the top of a greased slide and a big cell at the bottom."

"Maybe. At least the receiver would be behind bars."

"You could issue override cards to the police and other authorities, to let them shift in through a blockade."

"Good."

Whyte stopped suddenly, frowned. "There's a hole in it. A really big crowd would either wreck the station or smother, depending on how strong the cell was. Did you think of that?"

"I'd like to use more than one police station."

"How many? There's a distance limit . . . Barry, what are you thinking?"

"As it stands now, a long distance passenger has to dial three numbers to get anywhere. You said you could cut that to two. Can you cut it to one?"

"I don't know."

"It's poetic justice," said Jerryberry. "Our whole problem is that rioters can converge on one point from all over the United States. If we could use *police stations* all over the United States—we wouldn't have a problem. As soon as a cell was full here, we'd switch to police stations in San Diego or Oregon!"

Whyte was laughing. "If you could see your face! Barry, you're a dreamer."

"You can't do it."

"No, of course we can't do it. Wait a minute." Whyte pursed his lips. "There's a way. We could do it if there was a long distance receiver at the police station. Hook the network to a velocity damper! I told you, there's no reason you shouldn't be able to dial to a long distance receiver from *any* booth."

"It would work, then!"

"You'd have to talk the public into paying for it. Design wouldn't be much of a problem. We could cover the country with an emergency network in a couple of years."

"Can I quote you?"

"Of course. We sell displacement booths. That's our business."

X

Talk shows are one of the few remaining pure entertainment features on TV. With cassettes the viewer buys a package; with a talk show he never knows just what he's getting. It is a different product. It is cheap to produce. It can compete.

The *Tonight Show* shows at 8:30 PM, prime time.

Around nine they start flicking in, pouring out of the coin booths that line the street above the last row of houses. They mill about, searching out the narrow walks that lead down to the Strand. They pour over the low stone wall that guards the sand from the houses. They pause, awed.

Breakers roll in from the black sea, flashing electric blue.

Within minutes Hermosa Beach is aswarm with people. Men, women, children, in couples and family groups. They hold hands and look out to sea. They stamp the packed wet sand, dancing like savages, and whoop with delight to see blue light flash beneath their feet. High up on the dry sand are piles of discarded clothing. Swimmers are thick in the water, splashing blue fire at each other.

Many were drunk or high on this or that, when the *Tonight Show* led them here. Those who came were happy to start with. They came to do a happy thing. Some carry six-packs or pouches of pot.

The line of them stretches around the curve of the shore to the north, beyond Hermosa Pier to the south, bunching around the Pier. More are shifting-in all the time, trickling down to join the others.

Jerryberry Jansen flicked in almost an hour early for the interview.

The station was an ant's nest, a swarm of furious disorganization. Jerryberry was looking for Wash Evans when Wash Evans came running past him from behind, glanced back, came to a jarring halt.

" 'Lo," said Jerryberry. "Is there anything we need to go over before we go on?"

Evans seemed at a loss. "Yah," he said, and caught his breath a little, and said, "You're not news any more, Jansen. We may not even be doing the interview."

Jerryberry said a dirty word. "I *heard* they'd cleared up the riot—"

"More than that. They caught the lady shoplifter."

"Good!"

"If you say so. One out of a thousand people that recognized your pictures of her turned out to be right. Woman by the name of Irma Hennessey, lives in Jersey City but commutes all over the country. She says she's never hit the same store twice. She's a kick, Jansen. A newstaper's dream. No offense intended, but I wish they'd let her out of jail tonight. I'd interview *her*."

"So I didn't cause the Mall Riot any more, now you've got Irma Hennessey. Well, *good*. I didn't like being a celebrity. Anything else?"

He was thinking, *all that jumping around, all the things I learned today, all wasted. Unless I can get a tapezine lecture out of it—*

Evans said, "Yah. There's a new Mall Riot going on at Hermosa Beach."

"What the hell?"

"Craziest damn thing." Wash Evans lit a cigarette, talked around it. "You know Gordon Lundt, the 'zine star? He was on the *Tonight Show*, and he happened to mention the red tide down at Hermosa Beach. He said it was pretty. The next thing anyone knows, every man, woman and child in the country has decided he wants to see the red tide at Hermosa Beach."

"How bad is it?"

"Well, nobody's been hurt, last I heard. And they aren't breaking things. It's not that kind of crowd, and there's nothing to steal but sand, anyway. It's a happy riot, Jansen. There's just a bitch of a lot of people."

"Another flash crowd. It figures," said Jerryberry. "You can get a flash crowd anywhere there are displacement booths."

"Can you?"

"They've been around a long time. It's just that they happen faster with the long distance booths. Some places are permanent floating flash crowds. Like Tahiti. What's wrong?"

Wash Evans had a funny look. "It just hit me that we don't really have anything to replace you with. You've been doing your homework, have you?"

"All day." Jerryberry dug out the Minox. "I've been everywhere I could think of. Some of this goes with taped interviews." He produced the tape recorder. "Of course there isn't much time to sort it out—"

"No. Gimmee." Evans took the camera and the recorder. "We can follow up on these later. Maybe they'll make a special. Right now the news is at Hermosa Beach. And you sound like you know how it happened and what to do about it. Do you still want to do that interview?"

"I—sure."

"Go get a CBA camera from George Bailey. Let's see, it's—nine fifteen, dammit. Spend half an hour, see as much as you can, then get back here. Find out what you can about the—flash crowd at Hermosa Beach. That's what we'll be talking about."

George Bailey looked up as Jerryberry arrived. He pointed emphatically at the single camera remaining on

the table, finger-combed the hair back out of his eyes and
went back to monitoring half a dozen TV screens

The camera came satisfyingly to life in Jerryberry's
hands. He picked up a list of Hermosa Beach numbers
and turned to the displacement booths. Too much coffee
sloshed in his belly. He stopped suddenly, thinking:

One big riot control center would do it. You wouldn't
need a police network; just one long distance receiver to
serve the whole country, and a building the size of
Yankee Stadium, big enough to handle any riot. A federal
police force on permanent guard. Rioting was an inter-
state crime now anyway. You could build such a center
faster and cheaper than any network.

Not now. Back to work. He stepped into a booth,
dialed and was gone.

WHAT GOOD IS A GLASS DAGGER?

I

Twelve thousand years before the birth of Christ, in an age when miracles were somewhat more common, a warlock used an ancient secret to save his life.

In later years he regretted that. He had kept the secret of the Warlock's Wheel for several normal lifetimes. The demon-sword Glirendree and its stupid barbarian captive would have killed him, no question of that. But no mere demon could have been as dangerous as that secret.

Now it was out, spreading like ripples on a pond. The battle between Glirendree and the Warlock was too good a tale not to tell. Soon no man would call himself a magician who did not know that magic could be used up. So simple, so dangerous a secret. The wonder was that nobody had noticed it before.

A year after the battle with Glirendree, near the end of a summer day, Aran the Peacemonger came to Shayl Village to steal the Warlock's Wheel.

Aran was a skinny eighteen-year-old, lightly built. His face was lean and long, with a pointed chin. His dark eyes peered out from under a prominent shelf of bone. His short, straight dark hair dropped almost to his brows in a pronounced widow's peak. What he was was no secret;

and anyone who touched hands with him would have known at once, for there was short fine hair on his palms. But had anyone known his mission, he would have been thought mad.

For the Warlock was a leader in the Sorcerer's Guild. It was known that he had a name; but no human throat could pronounce it. The shadow demon who had been his name-father had later been imprisoned in tattooed runes on the Warlock's own back: an uncommonly dangerous bodyguard.

Yet Aran came well protected. The leather wallet that hung from his shoulder was old and scarred, and the seams were loose. By its look it held nuts and hard cheese and bread and almost no money. What it actually held was charms. Magic would serve him better than nuts and cheese, and Aran could feed himself as he traveled, at night.

He reached the Warlock's cave shortly after sunset. He had been told how to use his magic to circumvent the Warlock's safeguards. His need for magic implied a need for voice and hands, so that Aran was forced to keep the human shape; and this made him doubly nervous. At moonrise he chanted the words he had been taught, and drew a live bat from his pouch and tossed it gently through the barred entrance to the cave.

The bat exploded into a mist of blood that drifted slant-wise across the stone floor. Aran's stomach lurched. He almost ran then; but he quelled his fear and followed it in, squeezing between the bars.

Those who had sent him had repeatedly diagrammed the cave for him. He could have robbed it blindfolded. He would have preferred darkness to the flickering blue light from what seemed to be a captured lightning bolt tethered in the middle of the cavern. He moved quickly, scrupulously tracing what he had been told was a path of safety.

Though Aran had seen sorcerous tools in the training

laboratory in the School for Mercantile Grammaree in Atlantis, most of the Warlock's tools were unfamiliar. It was not an age of mass production. He paused by a workbench, wondering. Why would the Warlock be grinding a glass dagger?

But Aran found a tarnish-blackened metal disc hanging above the workbench, and the runes inscribed around its rim convinced him that it was what he had come for. He took it down and quickly strapped it against his thigh, leaving his hands free to fight if need be. He was turning to go, when a laughing voice spoke out of the air.

"Put that down, you mangy son of a bitch—"

Aran converted to wolf.

Agony seared his thigh!

In human form Aran was a lightly built boy. As a wolf he was formidably large and dangerous. It did him little good this time. The pain was blinding, stupefying. Aran the wolf screamed and tried to run from the pain.

He woke gradually, with an ache in his head and a greater agony in his thigh and a tightness at his wrists and ankles. It came to him that he must have knocked himself out against a wall.

He lay on his side with his eyes closed, giving no sign that he was awake. Gently he tried to pull his hands apart. He was bound, wrists and ankles. Well, he had been taught a word for unbinding ropes.

Best not to use it until he knew more.

He opened his eyes a slit.

The Warlock was beside him, seated in lotus position, studying Aran with a slight smile. In one hand he held a slender willow rod.

The Warlock was a tall man in robust good health. He was deeply tanned. Legend said that the Warlock never wore anything above the waist. The years seemed to blur on him; he might have been twenty or fifty. In fact he was one hundred and ninety years old, and bragged of it. His condition indicated the power of his magic.

Behind him, Aran saw that the Warlock's Wheel had been returned to its place on the wall.

Waiting for its next victim? The real Warlock's Wheel was of copper; those who had sent Aran had known that much. But this decoy must be tarnished silver, to have seared him so.

The Warlock wore a dreamy, absent look. There might still be a chance, if he could be taken by surprise. Aran said, "Kplir—"

The Warlock lashed him across the throat.

The willow wand had plenty of spring in it. Aran choked and gagged; he tossed his head, fighting for air.

"That word has four syllables," the Warlock informed him in a voice he recognized. "You'll never get it out."

"Gluck," said Aran.

"I want to know who sent you."

Aran did not answer, though he had his wind back.

"You're no ordinary thief. But you're no magician either," the Warlock said almost musingly. "I heard you. You were chanting by rote. You used basic spells, spells that are easy to get right, but they were the right spells each time.

"Somebody's been using prescience and farsight to spy on me. Someone knows too many of my defenses," the ancient magician said gently. "I don't like that. I want to know who, and why."

When Aran did not reply, the Warlock said, "He had all the knowledge, and he knew what he was after, but he had better sense than to come himself. He sent a fool." The Warlock was watching Aran's eyes. "Or perhaps he thought a werewolf would have a better chance at me. By the way, there's silver braid in those cords, so you'd best stay human for the nonce."

"You knew I was coming."

"Oh, I had ample warning. Didn't it occur to you that I've got prescience and farsight too? It occurred to your master," said the Warlock. "He set up protections around you, a moving region where prescience doesn't work."

"Then what went wrong?"

"I foresaw the dead region, you ninny. I couldn't get a glimpse of what was stealing into my cave. But I could look around it. I could follow its path through the cavern. That path was most direct. I knew what you were after.

"Then, there were bare footprints left behind. I could study them before they were made. You waited for moonrise instead of trying to get in after dusk. On a night of the full moon, too.

"Other than that, it wasn't a bad try. Sending a werewolf was bright. It would take a kid your size to squeeze between the bars, and then a kid your size couldn't win a fight if something went wrong. A wolf your size could."

"A lot of good it did me."

"What I want to know is, how did they talk an Atlantean into this? They must have known what they were after. Didn't they tell you what the Wheel does?"

"Sucks up magic," said Aran. He was chagrined, but not surprised, that the Warlock had placed his accent.

"Sucks up *mana*," the Warlock corrected him. "Do you know what *mana* is?"

"The power behind magic."

"So they taught you that much. Did they also tell you that when the *mana* is gone from a region, it doesn't come back? Ever?"

Aran rolled on his side. Being convinced that he was about to die, he felt he had nothing to lose by speaking boldly. "I don't understand why you'd want to keep it a secret. A thing like the Warlock's Wheel, it could make war obsolete! It's the greatest purely defensive weapon ever invented!"

The Warlock didn't seem to understand. Aran said, "You *must* have thought of that. Why, no enemy's curses could touch Atlantis, if the Warlock's Wheel were there to absorb it!"

"Obviously you weren't sent by the Atlantean Minister of Offense. He'd know better." The Warlock watched him shrewdly. "Or were you sent by the Greek Isles?"

"I don't understand."

"Don't you know that Atlantis is tectonically unstable? For the last half a thousand years, the only thing that's kept Atlantis above the waves has been the spells of the sorcerer-kings."

"You're lying."

"You obviously aren't." The Warlock made a gesture of dismissal. "But the Wheel would be bad for any nation, not just Atlantis. Spin the Wheel, and a wide area is dead to magic for—as far as I've been able to tell—the rest of eternity. Who would want to bring about such a thing?"

"I would."

"You would. Why?"

"We're sick of war," Aran said roughly. Unaware that he had said *we*. "The Warlock's Wheel would end war. Can you imagine an army trying to fight with nothing but swords and daggers? No hurling of death spells. No prescients spying out the enemy's battle plans. No killer demons beating at unseen protective walls." Aran's eyes glowed. "Man to man, sword against sword, blood and bronze, and no healing spells. Why, no king would ever fight on such terms! We'd give up war forever!"

"Some basic pessimism deep within me forces me to doubt it."

"You're laughing at me. You don't *want* to believe it," Aran said scornfully. "No more *mana* means the end of your youth spells. You'd be an old man, too old to live!"

"That must be it. Well, let's see who you are." The

Warlock touched Aran's wallet with the willow wand, let it rest there a few moments. Aran wondered frantically what the Warlock could learn from his wallet. If the lock-spells didn't hold, then—

They didn't, of course. The Warlock reached in, pulled out another live bat, then several sheets of parchment marked with what might have been geometry lessons and with script printed in a large, precise hand.

"Schoolboy script," he commented. "Lines drawn with painful accuracy, mistakes scraped out and redrawn . . . The idiot! He forgot the hooked tail on the Whirlpool design. A wonder it didn't eat him." The Warlock looked up. "Am I being attacked by children? These spells were prepared by half a dozen apprentices!"

Aran didn't answer; but he lost hope of concealing anything further.

"They have talent, though. So. You're a member of the Peacemongers, aren't you? All army-age youngsters. I'll wager you're backed by half the graduating class of the School of Mercantile Grammaree. They must have been watching me for months now, to have my defenses down so pat.

"And you want to end the war against the Greek Isles. Did you think you'd help matters by taking the Warlock's Wheel to Atlantis? Why, I'm half minded to let you walk out with the thing. It would serve you right for trying to rob me."

He looked hard into Aran's eyes. "Why, you'd do it, wouldn't you? Why? I said *why?*"

"We could still use it."

"You'd sink Atlantis. Are the Peacemongers traitors now?"

"I'm no traitor." Aran spoke low and furious. "We want to change Atlantis, not destroy it. But if we owned the Warlock's Wheel, the Palace would listen to us!"

He wriggled in his tight bonds, and thought once again

171

of the word that would free him. Then, convert to were-wolf and run! Between the bars, down the hill into the woods and freedom.

"I think I'll make a conservative of you," the Warlock said suddenly.

He stood up. He brushed the willow wand lightly across Aran's lips. Aran found that he could not open his mouth. He remembered now that he was entirely in the Warlock's power—and that he was a captured thief.

The Warlock turned, and Aran saw the design on his back. It was an elaborately curlicued five-sided tattoo in red and green and gold inks. Aran remembered what he had been told of the Warlock's bodyguard.

"Recently I dreamed," said the Warlock. "I dreamed that I would find a use for a glass dagger. I thought that the dream might be prophetic, and so I carved—"

"That's silly," Aran broke in. "What good is a glass dagger?"

He had noticed the dagger on the way in. It had a honed square point and honed edges and a fused-looking hilt with a guard. Two clamps padded with fox leather held it in place on the work table. The uppermost cutting edge was not yet finished.

Now the Warlock removed the dagger from its clamps. While Aran watched, the Warlock scratched designs on the blade with a pointed chunk of diamond that must have cost him dearly. He spoke low and softly to it, words that Aran couldn't hear. Then he picked it up like—a dagger.

Frightened as he was, Aran could not quite believe what the Warlock was doing. He felt like a sacrificial goat. There was *mana* in sacrifice . . . and more *mana* in human sacrifice . . . but he wouldn't. He wouldn't!

The Warlock raised the knife high, and brought it down hard in Aran's chest.

Aran screamed. He had felt it! A whisper of sensation, a slight ghostly tug—the knife was an insubstantial shadow. But there was a knife in Aran the Peace-monger's heart! The hilt stood up out of his chest!

The Warlock muttered low and fast. The glass hilt faded and was gone, apparently.

"It's easy to make glass invisible. Glass is half invisible already. It's still in your heart," said the Warlock. "But don't worry about it. Don't give it a thought. Nobody will notice. Only, be sure to spend the rest of your life in *mana*-rich territory. Because if you ever walk into a place where magic doesn't work—well, it'll reappear, that's all."

Aran struggled to open his mouth.

"Now, you came for the secret of the Warlock's Wheel, so you might as well have it. It's just a simple kinetic sorcery, but open-ended." He gave it. "The Wheel spins faster and faster until it's used all the *mana* in the area. It tends to tear itself apart, so you need another spell to hold it together—" and he gave that, speaking slowly and distinctly. Then he seemed to notice that Aran was flopping about like a fish. He said, "Kplirapranthry."

The ropes fell away. Aran stood up shakily. He found he could speak again, and what he said was, "Take it out. Please."

"Now, there's one thing about taking that secret back to Atlantis. I assume you still want to? But you'd have to describe it before you could use it as a threat. You can see how easy it is to make. A big nation like Atlantis tends to have enemies, doesn't it? And you'd be telling them how to sink Atlantis in a single night."

Aran pawed at his chest, but he could feel nothing. "Take it out."

"I don't think so. Now we face the same death, wolf boy. Goodby, and give my best to the School for Mercantile Grammaree. And, oh yes, don't go back by way of Hvirin Gap."

"Grandson of an ape!" Aran screamed. He would not beg again. He was wolf by the time he reached the bars, and he did not touch them going through. With his mind he felt the knife in his chest, and he heard the Warlock's laughter following him down the hill and into the trees.

When next he saw the Warlock, it was thirty years later and a thousand miles away.

II

Aran traveled as a wolf, when he could. It was an age of greater magic; a werewolf could change shape whenever the moon was in the sky. In the wolf shape Aran could forage, reserving his remaining coins to buy his way home.

His thoughts were a running curse against the Warlock.

Once he turned about on a small hill, and stood facing north toward Shayl Village. He bristled, remembering the Warlock's laugh; but he remembered the glass dagger. He visualized the Warlock's throat, and imagined the taste of arterial blood; but the glowing, twisting design on the Warlock's back flashed at the back of Aran's eyes, and Aran tasted defeat. He could not fight a shadow demon. Aran howled, once, and turned south.

Nildiss Range, the backbone of a continent, rose before him as he traveled. Beyond the Range was the sea, and a choice of boats to take him home with what he had learned of the Warlock. Perhaps the next thief would have better luck . . .

And so he came to Hvirin Gap.

Once the range had been a formidable barrier to trade. Then, almost a thousand years ago, a sorcerer of Rynildissen had worked an impressive magic. The Range had been split as if by a cleaver. Where the mountains to either side sloped precipitously upward, Hvirin Gap sloped smoothly down to the coast, between rock walls flat enough to have a polished look.

Periodically the bandits had to be cleaned out of Hvirin

Gap. This was more difficult every year; for the spells against banditry didn't work well there, and swords had to be used instead. The only compensation was that the dangerous mountain dragons had disappeared too.

Aran stopped at the opening. He sat on his haunches, considering.

For the Warlock might have been lying. He might have thought it funny to send Aran the long way over Nildiss Range.

But the dragon bones. Where magic didn't work, dragons died. The bones were there, huge and reptilian. They had fused with the rock of the pass somehow, so that they looked tens of millions of years old.

Aran had traveled the Gap in wolf form. If Hvirin Gap was dead to magic, he should have been forced into the man form. Or would he find it impossible to change at all?

"But I can go through as a wolf," Aran thought. "That way I can't be killed by anything but silver and platinum. The glass dagger should hurt, but—"

"Damn! I'm invulnerable, but is it *magic?* If it doesn't work in Hvirin Gap—" and he shuddered.

The dagger had never been more than a whisper of sensation, that had faded in half an hour and never returned. But Aran knew it was there. Invisible, a knife in his heart, waiting.

It might reappear in his chest, and he could still survive—as a wolf. But it would hurt! And he could never be human again.

Aran turned and padded away from Hvirin Gap. He had passed a village yesterday. Perhaps the resident magician could help him.

"A glass dagger!" the magician chortled. He was a portly, jolly, balding man, clearly used to good living. "Now I've heard everything. Well, what were you worried about? It's got a handle, doesn't it? Was it a complex spell?"

"I don't think so. He wrote runes on the blade, then stabbed me with it."

"Fine. You pay in advance. And you'd better convert to wolf, just to play safe." He named a sum that would have left Aran without money for passage home. Aran managed to argue him down to something not far above reason, and they went to work.

The magician gave up some six hours later. His voice was hoarse, his eyes were red from oddly colored, oddly scented smokes, and his hands were discolored with dyes. "I can't touch the hilt, I can't make it visible, I can't get any sign that it's there at all. If I use any stronger spell, it's likely to kill you. I quit, wolf boy. Whoever put this spell on you, he knows more than a simple village magician."

Aran rubbed at his chest where the skin was stained by mildly corrosive dyes. "They call him the Warlock."

The portly magician stiffened. "The Warlock? *The* Warlock? And you didn't think to tell me. Get out."

"What about my money?"

"I wouldn't have tried it for ten times the fee! Me, a mere hedge-magician, and you turned me loose against the Warlock! We might both have been killed. If you think you're entitled to your money, let's go to the headman and state our case. Otherwise, get out."

Aran left, shouting insults.

"Try other magicians if you like," the other shouted after him. "Try Rynildissen City! But tell them what they're doing first!"

III

It had been a difficult decision for the Warlock. But his secret was out and spreading. The best he could do was see to it that world sorcery understood the implications.

The Warlock addressed the Sorcerers' Guild on the subject of *mana* depletion and the Warlock's Wheel.

"Think of it every time you work magic," he thundered in what amounted to baby talk after his severely technical description of the Wheel. "Only finite *mana* in the world, and less of it every year, as a thousand magicians drain it away. There were beings who ruled the world as gods, long ago, until the raging power of their own being used up the *mana* that kept them alive.

"One day it'll all be gone. Then all the demons and dragons and unicorns, trolls and rocs and centaurs will vanish quite away, because their metabolism is partly based on magic. Then all the dream-castles will evaporate, and nobody will ever know they were there. Then all the magicians will become tinkers and smiths, and the world will be a dull place to live. You have the power to bring that day nearer!"

That night he dreamed.

A duel between magicians makes a fascinating tale. Such tales are common—and rarely true. The winner of such a duel is not likely to give up trade secrets. The loser is dead, at the very least.

Novices in sorcery are constantly amazed at how much preparation goes into a duel, and how little action. The duel with the Hill Magician started with a dream, the night after the Warlock's speech made that duel inevitable. It ended thirty years later.

In that dream the enemy did not appear. But the Warlock saw a cheerful, harmless-looking fairy castle perched on an impossible hill. From a fertile, hummocky landscape, the hill rose like a breaking wave, leaning so far that the castle at its crest had empty space below it.

In his sleep the Warlock frowned. Such a hill would topple without magic. The fool who built it was wasting *mana*.

And in his sleep he concentrated, memorizing details.

A narrow path curled up the hillside. Facts twisted, dreamlike. There was a companion with him; or there wasn't. The Warlock lived until he passed through the gate; or he died at the gate, in agony, with great ivory teeth grinding together through his rib cage.

He woke himself up trying to sort it out.

The shadowy companion was necessary, at least as far as the gate. Beyond the enemy's gate he could see nothing. A Warlock's Wheel must have been used there, to block his magic so thoroughly.

Poetic justice?

He spent three full days working spells to block the Hill Magician's prescient sense. During that time his own sleep was dreamless. The other's magic was as effective as his own.

IV

Great ships floated at anchor in the harbor.

There were cargo ships whose strange demonic figureheads had limited power of movement, just enough to reach the rats that tried to swarm up the mooring lines. A large Atlantean passenger liner was equipped with twin outriggers made from whole tree trunks. By the nearest dock a magician's slender yacht floated eerily above the water. Aran watched them all rather wistfully.

He had spent too much money traveling over the mountains. A week after his arrival in Rynildissen City he had taken a post as bodyguard/watchdog to a rug merchant. He had been down to his last coin, and hungry.

Now Lloraginezee the rug merchant and Ra-Harroo his secretary talked trade secrets with the captain of a Nile cargo ship. Aran waited on the dock, watching ships with indifferent patience.

His ears came to point. The bearded man walking past

him wore a captain's kilt. Aran hailed him: "Ho, Captain! Are you sailing to Atlantis?"

The bearded man frowned. "And what's that to you?"

"I would send a message there."

"Deal with a magician."

"I'd rather not," said Aran. He could hardly tell a magician that he wanted to send instructions on how to rob a magician. Otherwise the message would have gone months ago.

"I'll charge you more, and it will take longer," the bearded man said with some satisfaction. "Who in Atlantis, and where?"

Aran gave him an address in the city. He passed over the sealed message pouch he had been carrying for three months now.

Aran too had made some difficult decisions. In final draft his message warned of the tectonic instability of the continent, and suggested steps the Peacemongers could take to learn if the Warlock had lied. Aran had not included instructions for making a Warlock's Wheel.

Far out in the harbor, dolphins and mermen played rough and complicated games. The Atlantean craft hoisted sail. A wind rose from nowhere to fill the sails. It died slowly, following the passenger craft out to sea.

Soon enough, Aran would have the fare. He would almost have it now, except that he had twice paid out sorcerer's fees, with the result that the money was gone and the glass dagger was not. Meanwhile, Lloraginezee did not give trade secrets to his bodyguard. He knew that Aran would be on his way as soon as he had the money.

Here they came down the gangplank: Lloraginezee with less waddle than might be expected of a man of his girth; the girl walking with quiet grace, balancing the rug samples on her head. Ra-Harroo was saying something as Aran joined them, something Aran may have been intended to hear.

"Beginning tomorrow, I'll be off work for five days. *You* know," she told Lloraginezee—and blushed.

"Fine, fine," said Lloraginezee, nodding absently.

Aran knew too. He smiled but did not look at her. He might embarrass her . . . and he knew well enough what Ra-Harroo looked like. Her hair was black and short and coarse. Her nose was large but flat, almost merging into her face. Her eyes were brown and soft, her brows dark and thick. Her ears were delicately formed and convoluted, and came to a point. She was a lovely girl, especially to another of the wolf people.

They held hands as they walked. Her nails were narrow and strong, and the fine hair on her palm tickled.

In Atlantis he would have considered marrying her, had he the money to support her. Here, it was out of the question. For most of the month they were friends and co-workers. The night life of Rynildissen City was more convenient for a couple, and there were times when Lloraginezee could spare them both.

Perhaps Lloraginezee made such occasions. He was not of the wolf people. He probably enjoyed thinking that sex had reared its lovely, disturbing head. But sex could not be involved—except at a certain time of the month. Aran didn't see her then. She was locked up in her father's house. He didn't even know where she lived.

He found out five nights later.

He had guarded Lloraginezee's way to Adrienne's House of Pleasures. Lloraginezee would spend the night . . . on an air mattress floating on mercury, a bed Aran had only heard described. A pleasant sleep was not the least of pleasures.

The night was warm and balmy. Aran took a long way home, walking wide of the vacant lot behind Adrienne's. That broad, flat plot of ground had housed the palace of Shilbree the Dreamer, three hundred years ago. The palace had been all magic, and quite an achievement even in its day. Eventually it had . . . worn out, Shilbree would have said.

One day it was gone. And not even the simplest of spells would work in that vacant lot.

Someone had told Aran that households of wolf people occupied several blocks of the residential district. It seemed to be true, for he caught identifying smells as he crossed certain paths. He followed one, curious to see what kind of house a wealthy werewolf would build in Rynildissen.

The elusive scent led him past a high, angular house with a brass door . . . and then it was too late, for another scent was in his nostrils and in his blood and brain. He spent that whole night howling at the door. Nobody tried to stop him. The neighbors must have been used to it; or they may have known that he would kill rather than be driven away.

More than once he heard a yearning voice answering from high up in the house. It was Ra-Harroo's voice. With what remained of his mind, Aran knew that he would be finding apologies in a few days. She would think he had come deliberately.

Aran howled a song of sadness and deprivation and shame.

V

The first was a small village called Gath, and a Guild 'prentice who came seeking black opals. He found them, and free for the taking too, for Gath was dead empty. The 'prentice sorcerer wondered about that, and he looked about him, and presently he found a dead spot with a crumbled castle in it. It might have been a centurion fallen. Or it might have been raised by magic, and collapsed when the *mana* went out of it, yesterday or last week.

It was a queer tale, and it got around. The 'prentice grew rich on the opals, for black opals are very useful for cursing. But the empty village bothered him.

"I thought it was slavers at first," he said once, in the Warlock's hearing as it turned out. "There were no corpses, none anywhere. Slave traders don't kill if they can help it.

"But why would a troop of slavers leave valuables lying where they were? The opals were all over the street, mixed with hay. I think a jeweler must have been moving them in secret when—*something* smashed his wagon. But why didn't they pick up the jewels?"

It was the crumbled castle the Warlock remembered three years later, when he heard about Shiskabil. He heard of that one directly, from a magpie that fluttered out of the sky onto his shoulder and whispered, "Warlock?"

And when he had heard, he went.

Shiskabil was a village of stone houses within a stone wall. It must have been abandoned suddenly. Dinners had dried or rotted on their plates; meat had been burnt to ash in ovens. There were no living inhabitants, and no dead. The wall had not been breeched. But there were signs of violence everywhere: broken furniture, doors with broken locks or splintered hinges, crusted spears and swords and makeshift clubs, and blood. Dried black blood everywhere, as if it had rained blood.

Clubfoot was a younger Guild member, thin and earnest. Though talented, he was still a little afraid of the power he commanded through magic. He was not happy in Shiskabil. He walked with shoulders hunched, trying to avoid the places where blood had pooled.

"Weird, isn't it? But I had a special reason to send for you," he said. "There's a dead region outside the wall. I had the idea someone might have used a Warlock's Wheel there."

A rectangular plot of fertile ground, utterly dead, a foretaste of a world dead to magic. In the center were crumbled stones with green plants growing between.

The Warlock circled the place, unwilling to step where magic did not work. He had used the Wheel once before, against Glirendree, after the demon-sword had killed his shadow demon. The Wheel had sucked the youth from him, left the Warlock two hundred years old in a few seconds.

"There was magic worked in the village," said Clubfoot. "I tried a few simple spells. The *mana* level's very low. I don't remember any famous sorcerers from Shiskabil; do you?"

"No."

"Then whatever happened here was done by magic." Clubfoot almost whispered the word. Magic could be very evil—as he knew.

They found a zigzag path through the dead borderline, and a faintly live region inside. At a gesture from the Warlock, the crumbled stones stirred feebly, trying to rise.

"So it was somebody's castle," said Clubfoot. "I wonder how he got this effect?"

"I thought of something like it once. Say you put a heavy kinetic spell on a smaller Wheel. The Wheel would spin very fast, would use up mana in a very tight area—"

Clubfoot was nodding. "I see it. He could have run it on a track, a close path. It would give him a kind of hedge against magic around a live region."

"And he left the border open so he could get his tools in and out. He zigzagged the entrance so no spells could get through. Nobody could use farsight on him. I wonder . . ."

"I wonder what he had to hide?"

"I wonder what happened in Shiskabil," said the Warlock. And he remembered the dead barrier that hid the Hill Magician's castle. His leisurely duel with a faceless enemy was twelve years old.

It was twenty-three years old before they found the third village.

Hathzoril was bigger than Shiskabil, and better known. When a shipment of carvings in ivory and gem woods did not arrive, the Warlock heard of it.

The village could not have been abandoned more than a few days when the Warlock arrived. He and Clubfoot found meals half cooked, meals half eaten, broken furniture, weapons that had been taken from their racks, broken doors—

"But no blood. I wonder why?"

Clubfoot was jittery. "Otherwise it's just the same. The whole population gone in an instant, probably against their will. Ten whole years; no, more. I'd half forgotten . . . You got here before I did. Did you find a dead area and a crumbled castle?"

"No. I looked."

The younger magician rubbed his birth-maimed foot—which he could have cured in half an hour, but it would have robbed him of half his powers. "We could be wrong. If it's him, he's changed his techniques."

That night the Warlock dreamed a scrambled dream in pyrotechnic colors. He woke thinking of the Hill Magician.

"Let's climb some hills," he told Clubfoot in the morning. "I've got to know if the Hill Magician has something to do with these empty villages. We're looking for a dead spot on top of a hill."

That mistake almost killed him.

The last hill Clubfoot tried to climb was tumbled, crumbled soil and rock that slid and rolled under his

184

feet. He tried it near sunset, in sheer desperation, for they had run out of hills and patience.

He was still near the base when the Warlock came clambering to join him. "Come down from there!" he laughed. "Nobody would build on this sand heap."

Clubfoot looked around, and shouted, "Get out of here! You're older!"

The Warlock rubbed his face and felt the wrinkles. He picked his way back in haste and in care, wanting to hurry, but fearful of breaking fragile bones. He left a trail of fallen silver hair.

Once beyond the *mana*-poor region, he cackled in falsetto. "My mistake. I know what he did now. Clubfoot, we'll find the dead spot inside the hill."

"First we'll work you a rejuvenation spell." Clubfoot laid his tools out on a rock. A charcoal block, a silver knife, packets of leaves ...

"That border's bad. It sucks up *mana* from inside. He must have to move pretty often. So he raised up a hill like a breaking wave. When the magic ran out the hill just rolled over the castle and covered up everything. He'll do it again, too."

"Clever. What do you think happened in Hathzoril Village?"

"We may never know." The Warlock rubbed new wrinkles at the corners of his eyes. "Something bad, I think. Something very bad."

VI

He was strolling through the merchants' quarter that afternoon, looking at rugs.

Normally this was a cheerful task. Hanging rugs formed a brightly colored maze through this part of the quarter. As Aran the rug merchant moved through the maze, well-known voices would call his name. Then there would be gossip and canny trading.

He had traded in Rynildissen City for nearly thirty years, first as Lloraginezee's apprentice, later as his own man. The finest rugs and the cheapest, from all over this continent and nearby islands, came by ship and camel's back to Rynildissen City. Wholesalers, retailers, and the odd nobleman who wished to furnish a palace would travel to Rynildissen City to buy. Today they glowed in the hot sunlight . . . but today they only depressed him. Aran was thinking of moving away.

A bald man stepped into view from behind a block of cured sphinx pelts.

Bald as a roc's egg he was, yet young, and in the prime of muscular good health. He was shirtless like a stevedore, but his pantaloons were of high quality and his walk was pure arrogance. Aran felt he was staring rather rudely. Yet there was something familiar about the man.

He passed Aran without a glance.

Aran glanced back once, and was jolted. The design seemed to leap out at him: a five-sided multicolored tattoo on the man's back.

Aran called, "Warlock!"

He regretted it the next moment. The Warlock turned on him the look one gives a presumptuous stranger.

The Warlock had not changed at all, except for the loss of his hair. But Aran remembered that thirty years had passed; that he himself was a man of fifty, with the hollows of his face filled out by rich living. He remembered that his greying hair had receded, leaving his widow's peak as a shock of hair all alone on his forehead. And he remembered, in great detail, the circumstances under which he had met the Warlock.

He had spent a thousand nights plotting vengeance against the Warlock; yet now his only thought was to get away. He said, "Your pardon, sir—"

But something else occurred to him, so that he said firmly, "But we *have* met."

"Under what circumstance? I do not recall it," the Warlock said coldly.

Aran's answer was a measure of the self-confidence that comes with wealth and respect. He said, "I was robbing your cave."

"Were you!" The Warlock came closer. "Ah, the boy from Atlantis. Have you robbed any magicians lately?"

"I have adopted a somewhat safer way of life," Aran said equably. "And I do have reason for presuming on our brief acquaintance."

"Our brief—" The Warlock laughed so that heads turned all over the marketplace. Still laughing, he took Aran's arm and led him away.

They strolled slowly through the merchants' quarter, the Warlock leading. "I have to follow a certain path," he explained. "A project of my own. Well, my boy, what have you been doing for thirty years?"

"Trying to get rid of your glass dagger."

"Glass dagger? . . . Oh, yes, I remember. Surely you found time for other hobbies?"

Aran almost struck the Warlock then. But there was something he wanted from the Warlock; and so he held his temper.

"My whole life has been warped by your damned glass dagger," he said. "I had to circle Hvirin Gap on my way home. When I finally got here I was out of money. No money for passage to Atlantis, and no money to pay for a magician, which meant that I couldn't get the glass knife removed.

"So I hired out to Lloraginezee the rug merchant as a bodyguard/watchdog. Now I'm the leading rug merchant in Rynildissen City, I've got two wives and eight children and a few grandchildren, and I don't suppose I'll ever get back to Atlantis.

They bought wine from a peddler carrying two fat wineskins on his shoulders. They took turns drinking from the great copper goblet the man carried.

The Warlock asked, "Did you ever get rid of the knife?"

"No, and you ought to know it! What kind of a spell did you *put* on that thing? The best magicians in this continent haven't been able to so much as *touch* that knife, let alone pull it out. I wouldn't be a rug merchant if they had."

"Why not?"

"Well, I'd have earned my passage to Atlantis soon enough, except that every time I heard about a new magician in the vicinity I'd go to him to see if he could take that knife out. Selling rugs was a way to get the money to pay the magicians. Eventually I gave up on the magicians and kept the money. All I'd accomplished was to spread your reputation in all directions."

"Thank you," the Warlock said politely.

Aran did not like the Warlock's amusement. He decided to end the conversation quickly. "I'm glad we ran into each other," he said, "because I have a problem that is really in your province. Can you tell me something about a magician named Wavyhill?"

It may be that the Warlock stiffened. "What is it that you want to know?"

"Whether his spells use excessive power."

The Warlock lifted an interrogatory eyebrow.

"You see, we try to restrict the use of magic in Rynildissen City. The whole nation could suffer if a key region like Rynildissen City went dead to magic. There'd be no way to stop a flood, or a hurricane, or an invasion of barbarians. Do you find something amusing?"

"No, no. But could a glass dagger possibly have anything to do with your conservative attitude?"

"That's entirely my own business, Warlock. Unless you'd care to read my mind?"

"No, thank you. My apologies."

"I'd like to point out that more than just the welfare of Rynildissen City is involved. If this region went dead to magic, the harbor mermen would have to move away. They have quite an extensive city of their own, down there beyond the docks. Furthermore, they run most of the docking facilities and the *entire* fishing industry—"

"Relax. I agree with you completely. You know that," the magician laughed. "You ought to!"

"Sorry. I preach at the drop of a hat. It's been ten years since anyone saw a dragon near Rynildissen City. Even further out, they're warped, changed. When I first came here the dragons had a mercenary's booth in the city itself! What are you doing?"

The Warlock had handed the empty goblet back to the vendor and was pulling at Aran's arm. "Come this way, please. Quickly, before I lose the path."

"Path?"

"I'm following a fogged prescient vision. I could get killed if I lose the path—or if I don't, for that matter. Now, just what was your problem?"

"That," said Aran, pointing among the fruit stalls.

The troll was an ape's head on a human body, covered from head to toe in coarse brown hair. From its size it was probably female, but it had no more breasts than a female ape. It held a wicker basket in one quite human hand. Its bright brown eyes glanced up at Aran's pointing finger—startlingly human eyes—then dropped to the melon it was considering.

Perhaps the sight should have roused reverence. A troll was ancestral to humanity: *Homo habilis,* long extinct. But they were too common. Millions of the species had been fossilized in the drylands of Africa. Magicians of a few centuries ago had learned that they could be reconstituted by magic.

"I think you've just solved one of my own problems," the Warlock said quietly. He no longer showed any trace of amusement.

"Wonderful," Aran said without sincerity. "My own problem is, how much *mana* are Wavyhill's trolls using up? The *mana* level in Rynildissen City was never high to start with. Wavyhill must be using terrifically powerful spells just to keep them walking." Aran's fingertips brushed his chest in an unconscious gesture. "I'd hate to leave Rynildissen City, but if magic stops working here I won't have any choice."

"I'd have to know the spells involved. Tell me something about Wavyhill, will you? Everything you can remember."

To most of Rynildissen City the advent of Wavyhill the magician was very welcome.

Once upon a time troll servants had been common. They were terrifically strong. Suffering no pain, they could use hysterical strength for the most mundane tasks. Being inhuman, they could work on official holidays. They needed no sleep. They did not steal.

But Rynildissen City was old, and the *mana* was running low. For many years no troll had walked in Rynildissen City. At the gate they turned to blowing dust.

Then came Wavyhill with a seemingly endless supply of trolls, which did *not* disintegrate at the gate. The people paid him high prices in gold and in honors.

"For half a century thieves have worked freely on holidays," Aran told the Warlock. "Now we've got a trollish police force again. Can you blame people for being grateful? They made him a Councilman—over my objections. Which means that there's very little short of murder that Wavyhill can't do in Rynildissen City."

"I'm sorry to hear that. Why did you say *over your objections*? Are you on the Council?"

"Yes. I'm the one who rammed through the laws restricting magic in Rynildissen City. And failed to ram through some others, I might add. The trouble is that Wavyhill doesn't make the trolls in the city. Nobody knows where they come from. If he's depleting the *mana* level, he's doing it somewhere else."

"Then what's your problem?"

"Suppose the trolls use up *mana* just by existing? . . . I should be asking, *do they?*"

"I think so," said the Warlock.

"I *knew* it. Warlock, will you testify before the Council? Because——"

"No, I won't."

"But you've got to! I'll never convince anyone by myself. Wavyhill is the most respected magician around, and he'll be testifying against me! Besides which, the Council all own trolls themselves. They won't want to believe they've been suckered, and they have been if we're right. The trolls will collapse as soon as they've lowered the *mana* level enough."

At that point Aran ran down, for he had seen with what stony patience the Warlock was waiting for him to finish.

The Warlock waited three seconds longer, using silence as an exclamation point. Then he said, "It's gone beyond that. Talking to the Council would be like shouting obscenities at a forest fire. I could get results that way. You couldn't."

"Is he *that* dangerous?"

"I think so."

Aran wondered if he was being had. But the Warlock's face was so grave . . . and Aran had seen that face in too many nightmares. *What am I doing here?* he wondered. *I had a technical question about trolls. So I asked a magician . . . and now . . .*

"Keep talking. I need to know more about Wavyhill.

And walk faster," said the Warlock. "How long has he been here?"

"Wavyhill came to Rynildissen City seven years ago. Nobody knows where he came from; he doesn't have any particular accent. His palace sits on a hill that looks like it's about to fall over. What are you nodding at?"

"I know that hill. Keep talking."

"We don't see him often. He comes with a troupe of trolls, to sell them; or he comes to vote with the Council on important matters. He's short and dark——."

"That could be a seeming. Never mind, describe him anyway. I've never seen him."

"Short and dark, with a pointed nose and a pointed chin and very curly dark hair. He wears a dark robe of some soft material, a tall pointed hat, and sandals, and he carries a sword."

"Does he!" The Warlock laughed out loud.

"What's the joke? I carry a sword myself sometimes. —Oh, that's right, magicians have a *thing* about swordsmen."

"That's not why I laughed. It's a trade joke. A sword can be a symbol of masculine virility."

"Oh?"

"You see the point, don't you? A sorcerer doesn't need a sword. He knows more powerful protections. When a sorcerer takes to carrying a sword, it's pretty plain he's using it as a cure for impotence."

"And it works?"

"Of course it works. It's straight one-for-one similarity magic, isn't it? But you've got to take the sword to bed with you!" laughed the Warlock. But his eyes found a troll servant, and his laughter slipped oddly.

He watched as the troll hurried through a gate in a high white wall. They had passed out of the merchants' quarter.

"I think Wavyhill's a necromancer," he said abruptly.

"Necromancer. What is it? It sounds ugly."

"A technical term for a new branch of magic. And it is ugly. Turn sharp left here."

They ducked into a narrow alley. Two- and three-story houses leaned over them from both sides. The floor of the alley was filthy, until the Warlock snarled and gestured. Then the dirt and garbage flowed to both sides.

The Warlock hurried them deep into the alley. "We can stop here, I think. Sit down if you like. We'll be here for some time—or I will."

"Warlock, are you playing games with me? What does this new dance have to do with a duel of sorcery?"

"A fair question. Do you know what lies that way?"

Aran's sense of direction was good, and he knew the city. "The Judging Place?"

"Right. And that way, the vacant lot just this side of Adrienne's House of Pleasures—you know it? The deadest spot in Rynildissen City. The palace of Shilbree the Dreamer once stood there."

"*Might* I ask—"

"The courthouse is void of *mana* too, naturally. Ten thousand defendants and thirty thousand lawyers all praying for conviction or acquittal doesn't leave much magic in *any* courthouse. If I can keep either of those spots between me and Wavyhill, I can keep him from using farsight on me."

Aran thought about it. "But you have to know where he is."

"No. I only have to know where I ought to be. Most of the time, I don't. Wavyhill and I have managed to fog each other's prescient senses pretty well. But I'm supposed to be meeting an unknown ally along about now, and I've taken great care that Wavyhill can't spy on me.

"You see, I invented the Wheel. Wavyhill has taken the Wheel concept and improved it in at least two ways that I know of. Naturally he uses up *mana* at a ferocious rate.

"He may also be a mass murderer. And he's my fault. That's why I've got to kill him."

Aran remembered then that his wives were waiting dinner. He remembered that he had decided to end this conversation hours ago. And he remembered a story he had been told, of a layman caught in a sorcerer's duel, and what had befallen him.

"Well, I've got to be going," he said, standing up. "I wish you the best of luck in your duel, Warlock. And if there's anything I can do to help . . ."

"Fight with me," the Warlock said instantly.

Aran gaped. Then he burst out laughing.

The Warlock waited with his own abnormal patience. When he had some chance of being heard, he said, "I dreamed that an ally would meet me during this time. That ally would accompany me to the gate of Wavyhill's castle. I don't have many of those dreams to help me, Aran. Wavyhill's good. If I go alone, my forecast is that I'll be killed."

"Another ally," Aran suggested.

"No. Too late. The time has passed."

"Look." Aran slapped his belly with the flat of his hand. The flesh rippled. "It's not that much extra weight," he said, "for a man. I'm not *unsightly*. But as a wolf I'd look ten years pregnant! I haven't turned wolf in years.

"What am I doing? I don't have to convince you of anything," Aran said abruptly. And he walked away fast.

The Warlock caught him up at the mouth of the alley. "I swear you won't regret staying. There's something you don't know yet."

"Don't follow me too far, Warlock. You'll lose your path." Aran laughed in the magician's face. "Why should I fight by your side? If you really need me to win, I couldn't be more delighted! I've seen your face in a thousand nightmares, you and your glass dagger! So die, Warlock. It's my dinner time."

"Shh," said the Warlock. And Aran saw that the Warlock was not looking at him, but over his shoulder.

Aran felt the urge to murder. But his eyes flicked to follow the Warlock's gaze, and the imprecations died in his throat.

It was a troll. Only a troll, a male, with a tremendous pack on its back. Coming toward them.

And the Warlock was gesturing to it. Or were those magical passes?

"Good," he said. "Now, I could tell you that it's futile to fight fate, and you might even believe me, because I'm an expert. But I'd be lying. Or I could offer you a chance to get rid of the dagger—"

"Go to Hell. I learned to live with that dagger—"

"Wolf man, if you never learn anything else from me, learn never to blaspheme in the presence of a magician! Excuse me." The troll had walked straight to the mouth of the alley. Now the Warlock took it by the arm and led it inside. "Will you help me? I want to get the pack off its back."

They lifted it down, while Aran wondered at himself. Had he been bewitched into obedience? The pack was very heavy. It took all of Aran's strength, even though the Warlock bore the brunt of the load. The troll watched them with blank brown eyes.

"Good. If I tried this anywhere else in the city, Wavy-hill would know it. But this time I know where he is. He's in Adrienne's House of Pleasures, searching for me, the fool! He's already searched the courthouse.

"Never mind that. Do you know of a village named Gath?"

"No."

"Or Shiskabil?"

"No. Wait." A Shiska had bought six matching green rugs from him once. "Yes. A small village north of here. Something . . . happened to it . . ."

"The population walked out one night, leaving all their valuables and a good deal of unexplained blood."

"That's right." Aran felt sudden horrible doubt. "It was never explained."

"Gath was first. Then Shiskabil, then Hathzoril. Bigger cities each time. At Hathzoril he was clever. He found a way to hide where his palace had been, and he didn't leave any blood."

"But what does he *do?* Where do the people go?"

"What do you know about *mana,* Aran? You know that it's the power behind magic, and you know it can be used up. What else?"

"I'm not a magician. I sell rugs."

"*Mana* can be used for good or evil; it can be drained, or transferred from one object to another, or from one man to another. Some men seem to carry *mana* with them. You can find concentrations in oddly shaped stones, or in objects of reverence, or in meteoroids.

"There is much *mana* associated with murder," said the Warlock. "Too much for safety, in my day. My teacher used to warn us against working near the site of a murder, or the corpse of a murdered man, or murder weapons—as opposed to weapons of war, I might add. War and murder are different in intent.

"Necromancy uses murder as a source of magic. It's the most powerful form of magic—so powerful that it could never have developed until now, when the *mana* level everywhere in the world is so low.

"I think Wavyhill is a necromancer," said the Warlock. And he turned to the troll. "We'll know in a moment."

The troll stood passive, its long arms relaxed at its sides, watching the Warlock with strangely human brown eyes and with a human dignity that contrasted oddly with its low animal brow and hairy body. It did not flinch as the Warlock dropped a kind of necklace over its head.

The change came instantly. Aran backed away, sucking air. The Warlock's necklace hung around a man's neck—a man in his middle thirties, blond-haired and bearded, wearing a porter's kilt—and that man's belly had been cut wide open by one clean swing of a sword or scimitar. Aran caught the smell of him: he had been dead for three or four days, plus whatever time the preserving effects of magic had been at work on him. Yet he stood, passively waiting, and his expression had not changed.

"Wavyhill has invented a kind of perpetual motion," the Warlock said dryly; but he backed away hastily from the smell of the dead man. "There's enough power in a murdered man to make him an obedient slave, and plenty left over to cast on him the seeming of a troll. He takes more *mana* from the environment, but what of that? When the *mana* runs out in Gath, Wavyhill's trolls kill their masters. Then twice as many trolls move on to Shiskabil. In Hathzoril they probably used strangling cords; they wouldn't spill any blood that way, and they wouldn't bleed themselves. I wonder where he'll go after Rynildissen?"

"Nowhere! We'll tell the Council!"

"And Wavyhill a Councilman? No. And you can't spread the word to individual members, because eventually one of them would tip Wavyhill that you're slandering him."

"They'd believe *you*."

"All it takes is one who doesn't. Then he tells Wavyhill, and Wavyhill turns loose the trolls. No. You'll do three things," said the Warlock in tones not of command but of prophecy. "You'll go home. You'll spend the next week getting your wives and children out of Rynildissen City."

"My gods, yes!"

"I swore you wouldn't regret hearing me out. The third thing, if you so decide, is to join me at dawn, at the north gate, a week from today. Come by way of Adrienne's House of Pleasures," the Warlock ordered, "and stay awhile. The dead area will break your trail.

"Do that today, too. I don't want Wavyhill to follow you by prescience. Go now," said the Warlock.

"I can't decide!"

"Take a week."

"I may not be here. How can I contact you?"

"You can't. It doesn't matter. I'll go with you or without you." Abruptly the Warlock stripped the necklace from the neck of the standing corpse, turned and strode off down the alley. Following the path.

The dead man was a troll again. It followed Aran with large, disturbingly human brown eyes.

VII

That predawn morning, Adrienne's House of Pleasures was wrapped in thick black fog. Aran the rug merchant hesitated at the door; then, shivering, squared his shoulders and walked out into it.

He walked with his sword ready for tapping or killing. The fog grew lighter as he went, but no less dense. Several times he thought he saw monstrous vague shapes pacing him. But there was no attack. At dawn he was at the north gate.

The Warlock's mounts were either lizards enlarged by magic or dragons mutated by no magic. They were freaks, big as twin bungalows. One carried baggage; the other, two saddles in tandem.

"Mount up," the Warlock urged. "We want to get there before nightfall." Despite the chill of morning he was bare to the waist. He turned in his saddle as Aran settled behind him. "Have you lost weight?"

"I fasted for six days, and exercised too. And my wives and children are four days on their way to Atlantis by sea. You can guess what pleasures I chose at Adrienne's."

"I wouldn't have believed it. Your belly's as flat as a board."

"A wolf can fast for a long time. I ate an unbelievable meal last night. Today I won't eat at all."

The fog cleared as they left Rynildissen, and the morning turned clear and bright and hot. When Aran mentioned it, the Warlock said, "That fog was mine. I wanted to blur things for Wavyhill."

"I thought I saw shapes in the fog. Were those yours too?"

"No."

"Thanks."

"Wavyhill meant to frighten you, Aran. He wouldn't attack you. He *knows* you won't be killed before we reach the gate."

"That explains the pack lizards. I wondered how you could possibly expect to sneak up on him."

"I don't. He knows we're coming. He's waiting."

The land was rich in magic near Wavyhill's castle. You could tell by the vegetation: giant mushrooms, vying for variety of shape and color; lichens growing in the shapes of men or beasts; trees with contorted trunks and branches, trees that moved menacingly as the pack-lizards came near.

"I could make them talk," said the Warlock. "But I couldn't trust them. They'll be Wavyhill's allies."

In the red light of sunset, Wavyhill's castle seemed all rose marble, perched at the top of a fairy mountain. The slender tower seemed made for kidnapped damsels. The mountain itself, as Aran saw it now for the first time, was less a breaking wave than a fist raised to the sky in defiance.

"We couldn't use the Wheel here," said the Warlock. "The whole mountain would fall on us."

"I wouldn't have let you use the Wheel."

"I didn't bring one."

"Which way?"

"Up the path. He knows we're coming."

"Is your shadow demon ready?"

"Shadow demon?" The Warlock seemed to think. "Oh. For a moment I didn't know what you were talking about. That shadow demon was killed in the battle with Glirendree, thirty years ago."

Words caught in Aran's throat, then broke loose in a snarl. *"Then why don't you put on a shirt?"*

"Habit. I've got lots of strange habits. Why so vehement?"

"I don't know. I've been staring at your back since morning. I guess I was counting on the shadow demon." Aran swallowed. "It's just us, then?"

"Just us."

"Aren't you even going to take a sword? Or a dagger?"

"No. Shall we go?"

The other side of the hill was a sixty degree slope. The narrow, meandering path could not support the lizard beasts. Aran and the Warlock dismounted and began to climb.

The Warlock said, "There's no point in subtlety. We know we'll get as far as the gate. So does Wavyhill . . . excuse me." He threw a handful of silver dust ahead of them. "The road was about to throw us off. Apparently Wavyhill doesn't take anything for granted."

But Aran had only the Warlock's word for it; and that was the only danger that threatened their climb.

There was a rectangular pond blocking the solid copper gates. An arched bridge led across the pond. They were approaching the bridge when their first challenger pushed between the gates.

"What is it?" Aran whispered. "I've never *heard* of anything like it."

"There isn't. It's a changed one. Call it a snail dragon. . ."

. . . A snail dragon. Its spiral shell was just wide enough to block the gate completely. Its slender, supple body was fully exposed, reared high to study the intruders. Shiny leaflike scales covered the head and neck; but the rest of the body was naked, a soft greyish-brown. Its eyes were like black marbles. Its teeth were white and pointed, and the longest pair had been polished to a liquid glow.

From the other side of the small arched bridge, the Warlock called, "Ho, guardian! Were you told of our coming?"

"No," said the dragon. "Were you welcome, I would have been told."

"Welcome!" The Warlock guffawed. "We came to kill your master. Now, the interesting thing is that he knows of our coming. Why did he not warn you?"

The snail dragon tilted its mailed head.

The Warlock answered himself. "He knows that we will pass this gate. He suspects that we must pass over your dead body. He chose not to tell you so."

"That was kind of him." The dragon's voice was low and very gravelly, a sound like rocks being crushed.

"Kind, yes. But since we are foredoomed to pass, why not step aside? Or make for the hills, and we will keep your secret."

"It cannot be."

"You're a changed one, snail dragon. Beasts whose energy of life is partly magical, breed oddly where the *mana* is low. Most changed ones are not viable. So it is with you," said the Warlock. "The shell could not protect you from a determined and patient enemy. Or were you counting on speed to save you?"

"You raise a salient point," said the guardian. "If I

were to leave now, what then? My master will very probably kill you when you reach his sanctum. Then, by and by, this week or the next, he will wonder how you came to pass his guardian. Then, next week or the week following, he will come to see, or to remove the discarded shell. By then, with luck and a good tail wind, I could be halfway to the woods. Perchance he will miss me in the tall grass," said the bungalow-sized beast. "No. Better to take my chances here in the gate. At least I know the direction of attack."

"Damn, you're right," said the Warlock. "My sympathies, snail dragon."

And he set about fixing the bridge into solidity. Half of it, the half on the side away from the gate, really was solid. The other half was a reflected illusion, until the Warlock—did things.

"The dead border runs under the water," he told Aran. "Don't fall into it."

The snail dragon withdrew most of itself into its shell. Only his scaly head showed now, as Aran and the Warlock crossed.

Aran came running.

He was still a man. It was not certain that Wavyhill knew that Aran was a werewolf. It *was* certain that they would pass the gate. So he reserved his last defense, and came at the dragon with a naked sword.

The dragon blew fire.

Aran went through it. He carried a charm against dragon fire.

But he couldn't *see* through it. It shocked hell out of him when teeth closed on his shoulder. The dragon had stretched incredibly. Aran screamed and bounced his blade off the metallic scales and—the teeth loosed him, snapped ineffectually at the Warlock, who danced back laughing, waving—

But the Warlock had been unarmed!

The dragon collapsed. His thick neck was cut half in

two, behind the scales. The Warlock wiped his weapon on his pantaloons and held it up.

Aran felt suddenly queasy.

The Warlock laughed again. " 'What good is a glass dagger?' The fun thing about being a magician is that everyone always expects you to use magic."

"But, but—"

"It's just a glass dagger. No spells on it, nothing Wavyhill could detect. I had a friend drop it in the pond two days ago. Glass in water is near enough to invisible to fool the likes of Wavyhill."

"Excuse my open mouth. I just don't like glass daggers. Now what?"

The corpse and shell of the snail dragon still blocked the gate.

"If we try to squeeze around, we could be trapped. I suppose we'll have to go over."

"Fast," said Aran.

"Right, fast. Keep in mind that he could be *anywhere.*" The Warlock took a running start and ran/climbed up the curve of the shell.

Aran followed almost as quickly.

In his sanctum, the snail dragon had said. The picture he had evoked was still with Aran as he went up the shell. Wavyhill would be hidden in his basement or his tower room, in some place of safety. Aran and the Warlock would have to fight their way through whatever the enemy could raise against them, while Wavyhill watched to gauge their defenses. There were similar tales of magicians' battles . . .

Aran was ravenously hungry. It gave him a driving energy he hadn't had in years, decades. His pumping legs drove a body that seemed feather-light. He reached the top of the shell just as the Warlock was turning full about in apparent panic.

Then he saw them: a horde of armed and armored skeletons coming at them up a wooden plank. There must have been several score of them. Aran shouted and drew his sword. *How do you kill a skeleton?*

The Warlock shouted too. Strange words, in the Guild language.

The skeletons howled. A whirlwind seemed to grip them and lift them and fling them forward. Already they were losing form, like smoke rings. Aran turned to see the last of them vanishing into the Warlock's back.

My name is legion. They must have been animated by a single demon. And the Warlock had pulled that demon into a demon trap, empty and waiting for thirty years.

The problem was that both Aran and the Warlock had been concentrating on the plural demon.

The Warlock's back was turned, and Aran could do nothing. He spotted Wavyhill gesticulating from across the courtyard, in the instant before Wavyhill completed his spell.

Aran turned to shout a warning; and so he saw what the spell did to the Warlock. The Warlock was old in an instant. The flesh seemed to fade into his bones. He looked bewildered, spat a mouthful of blackened pebbles —no, teeth—closed his eyes and started to fall.

Aran caught him.

It was like catching an armload of bones. He eased the Warlock onto his back on the great snail shell. The Warlock's breathing was stertorous; he could not have long to live.

"Aran the Merchant!"

Aran looked down. "What did you do to him?"

The magician Wavyhill was dressed as usual, in dark robe and sandals and pointed hat. A belt with a shoulder loop held his big-hilted sword just clear of the ground. He called, "That is precisely what I wish to discuss. I have found an incantation that behaves as the Warlock's Wheel behaves, but directionally. Is this over your head?"

"I understand you."

"In layman's terms, I've sucked the magic from him.

That leaves him two hundred and twenty-six years old. I believe that gives me the win."

"My problem is whether to let you live. Aran, do you understand what my spell will do to you?"

Aran did, but—"Tell me anyway. Then tell me how you found out."

"From some of my colleagues, of course, after I determined that you were my enemy. You must have consulted an incredible number of magicians regarding the ghostly knife in your heart."

"More than a dozen. Well?"

"Leave in peace. Don't come back."

"I have to take the Warlock."

"He is my enemy."

"He's my ally. I won't leave him," said Aran.

"Take him then."

Aran stooped. He was forty-eight years old, and the bitterness of defeat had replaced the manic energy of battle. But the Warlock was little more than a snoring mummy, dry and light. The problem would be to get the fragile old man down from the snail shell.

Wavyhill was chanting!

Aran stood—in time to see the final gesture. Then the spell hit him.

For an instant he thought that the knife had truly reappeared in his heart. But the pain was all through him! like a million taut strings snapping inside him! The shape of his neck changed grindingly; all of his legs snapped forward; his skull flattened, his eyes lost color vision, his nose stretched, his lips pulled back from bared teeth.

The change had never come so fast, had never been more complete. A blackness fell on Aran's mind. It was a wolf that rolled helplessly off the giant snail shell and into the courtyard. A wolf bounced heavily and rolled to its feet, snarled deep in its throat and began walking stiff-legged toward Wavyhill.

Wavyhill was amazed! He started the incantation over, speaking very fast, as Aran approached. He finished as Aran came within leaping distance.

This time there was no change at all. Except that Aran leapt, and Wavyhill jumped back just short of far enough, and Aran tore his throat out.

For Aran the nightmare began then. What had gone before was as sweet dreams.

Wavyhill should have been dead. His severed carotid arteries pumped frantically, his windpipe made horrid bubbling sounds, and—Wavyhill drew his sword and attacked.

Aran the wolf circled and moved in and slashed—and backed away howling, for Wavyhill's sword had run him through the heart. The wound healed instantly. Aran the wolf was not surprised. He leapt away, and circled, and slashed and was stabbed again, and circled . . .

It went on and on.

Wavyhill's blood had stopped flowing. He'd run out. Yet he was still alive. So was his sword, or so it seemed. Aran never attacked unless it seemed safe, but the sword bit him every time. And every time he attacked, he came away with a mouthful of Wavyhill.

He was going to win. He could not help but win. His wounds healed as fast as they were made. Wavyhill's did not. Aran was stripping the flesh from the magician's bones.

There was a darkness on his brain. He moved by animal cunning. Again and again he herded Wavyhill back onto the slippery flagstones where Wavyhill had spilled five quarts of his blood. Four feet were surer than two. It was that cunning that led him to bar Wavyhill from leaving the courtyard. He tried. He must have stored healing magic somewhere in the castle. But Aran would not let him reach it.

He had done something to himself that would not let

him die. He must be regretting it terribly. Aran the wolf had crippled him now, slashing at his ankles until there was not a shred of muscle left to work the bones. Wavyhill was fighting on his knees. Now Aran came closer, suffering the bite of the sword to reach the magician . . .

Nightmare.

Aran the Peacemonger had been wrong. If Aran the rug merchant could work on and on, stripping the living flesh from a man in agony, taking a stab wound for every bite—if Aran could suffer such agonies to do this to *anyone,* for *any* cause—

Then neither the end of magic, nor anything else, would ever persuade men to give up war. They would fight on, with swords and stones and whatever they could find, for as long as there were men.

The blackness had lifted from Aran's brain. It must have been the sword: the *mana* in an enchanted sword had replaced the *mana* sucked from him by Wavyhill's variant of the Warlock's Wheel.

And, finally, he realized that the sword was fighting alone.

Wavyhill was little more than bloody bones. He might not be dead, but he certainly couldn't move. The sword waved itself at the end of the stripped bones of his arm, still trying to keep Aran away.

Aran slid past the blade. He gripped the hilt in his teeth and pulled it from the magician's still-fleshy hand. The hand fought back with a senseless determined grip, but it wasn't enough.

He had to convert to human to climb the dragon shell.

The Warlock was still alive, but his breathing was a thing of desperation. Aran laid the blade across the Warlock's body and waited.

The Warlock grew young. Not as young as he had been, But he no longer looked—dead. He was in the neighborhood of seventy years old when he opened his eyes, blinked, and asked, "What happened?"

"You missed all the excitement," said Aran.

"I take it you beat him. My apologies. It's been thirty years since I fought Glirendree. With every magician in the civilized world trying to duplicate the Warlock's Wheel, one or another was bound to improve on the design."

"He used it on me, too."

"Oh?" The Warlock chuckled. "I suppose you're wondering about the knife."

"It did come to mind. Where is it?"

"In my belt. Did you think I'd leave it in your chest? I'd had a dream that I would need it. So I kept it. And sure enough—"

"But it was in my heart!"

"I made an image of it. I put the image in your heart, then faded it out."

Aran's fingernails raked his chest. "You miserable son of an ape! You let me think that knife was in me for thirty years!"

"You came to my house as a thief," the Warlock reminded him. "Not an invited guest."

Aran the merchant had acquired somewhat the same attitude toward thieves. With diminished bitterness he said, "Just a little magician's joke, was it? No wonder nobody could get it out. All right. Now tell me why Wavyhill's spell turned me into a wolf."

The Warlock sat up carefully. He said, "What?"

"He waved his arms at me and sucked all the *mana* out of me, and I turned into a wolf. I even lost my human intelligence. Probably my invulnerability too. If he hadn't been using an enchanted sword he'd have cut me to ribbons."

"I don't understand that. You should have been frozen into human form. Unless . . . ."

Then, visibly, the answer hit him. His pale cheeks paled

further. Presently he said, "You're not going to like this, Aran."

Aran could see it in the Warlock's face, seventy years old and very tired and full of pity. "Go on," he said.

"The Wheel is a new thing. Even the dead spots aren't *that* old. The situation has never come up before, that's all. People automatically assume that werewolves are people who can turn themselves into wolves.

"It seems obvious enough. You can't even make the change without moonlight. You keep your human intelligence. But there's never been proof, one way or another, until now."

"You're saying I'm a wolf."

"Without magic, you're a wolf," the Warlock agreed.

"Does it matter? I've spent most of my life as a man," Aran whispered. "What difference does it make—oh. Oh, yes."

"It wouldn't matter if you didn't have children."

"Eight. And they'll have children. And one day the *mana* will be gone everywhere on Earth. Then what, Warlock?"

"You know already."

"They'll be wild dogs for the rest of eternity!"

"And nothing anyone can do about it."

"Oh, yes, there is! I'm going to see to it that no magician ever enters Rynildissen again!" Aran stood up on the dragon's shell. "Do you hear me, Warlock? Your kind will be barred. Magic will be barred. We'll save the *mana* for the sea people and the dragons!"

It may be that he succeeded. Fourteen thousand years later, there are still tales of werewolves where Rynildissen City once stood. Certainly there are no magicians.

AFTERWORD

A word about how these stories came to be written.

I had been claiming that time travel is fantasy as opposed to science fiction; that is, time travel is clearly impossible on any level. One morning it hit me that if time travel is fantasy, then a working time machine would . . . and the result was "Get a Horse!", retitled "The Flight of the Horse." I outlined the story that afternoon, and *told* it to some people at a cocktail party that night.

A good test for a story idea: if you can tell it standing up without confusing yourself, confusing your listener, or losing his interest, it's a story worth writing. I used to bend my brother's ear constantly. Now I can generally judge a story without that test. (But thanks, Mike.)

But I told all of the Svetz stories before I wrote them. The theme is fun to play games with. See, the extension cage is a *fantasy* vehicle, and Svetz doesn't know it . . .

One thing about fantasy: a fantasy story self-admittedly has no connection with any specific reality. Thus the writer is obligated to talk in universals. Otherwise he's not talking about anything. (One can ignore any obligation, of course.)

It took me a good long time to learn how to write fantasy. Primarily I write science fiction. *Glass Dagger* is my only swords-and-sorcery novelette, to date and possibly forever.

I hate writing for deadlines. I've only done it twice in my life, both times for Bob Silverberg's anthologies. He can tell you what happened the first time, when I promised him a Pluto story for *Tomorrow's Worlds*.

With two weeks to his deadline, I had already written him a letter saying that he couldn't have the story, sorry, I only had half an idea and two weeks wasn't enough. The letter was sitting on my hi-fi set, waiting to be mailed, when I got the other half of the idea. Bob got a *tiny* story, practically a vignette, and he got it at the last possible moment.

There was no such problem with "Flash Crowd," I'm happy to say. Except that my wife, who remembers that occasion, kept nudging me to sit down and *write* it. Nagging, nagging, always nagging. I turned the story in *days* early.

And the notes left over leave room for a whole series of stories dealing with a society moulded by teleportation. Someday I'll write it.